# STORMS OVER BABYLON

Jennifer Macaire

Published by Accent Press Ltd 2018
Octavo House
West Bute Street
Cardiff
CF10 5LJ

www.accentpress.co.uk

ISBN 9781786154828
eISBN 9781786154620

*"This man, it was I who saved him when he was shipwrecked, alone in the storm, after Zeus capsized and destroyed his vessel as it sailed in the wine-coloured sea ..." Calypso*

Homer, "The Odyssey"

*"O, Athenians, can you believe what dangers I've affronted just to merit your praises?"*

Onesicritus: Alexander to his generals

*"Shāh Māt" – Checkmate – The king is dead.*

# Chapter One

'Is it always going to be like this?'

'Like what?'

I turned my head and looked at my husband. He was lying on his side next to me, his hands clasped behind his head. From outside the tent came the usual commotion and clamour of forty thousand soldiers, hundreds of horses, sundry slaves, countless cooks, dozens of doctors, and whoever else made up the army. Inside, it was peaceful - Chiron was napping.

Alexander nodded his chin towards the tent flap. Sunlight flooded in showing motes of dust floating in the air. 'There's plenty of water. The air is dry, but the bushes give many berries and there is a great quantity of hares that my soldiers love to eat.'

'Are you asking me if the voyage is going to go this smoothly all the time?' I leaned up on my elbow and stared at him.

He grinned. 'Why not? I can ask my own oracle, can't I?'

I narrowed my eyes and shook my head slowly. 'Oh no you don't. I won't say a bloody thing, Alexander. You don't think I'm going to tell you everything that's going to happen, do you? Besides,' I flopped back on the bed, 'I have no idea. I already told you, I'm not an expert on you.

Anyway, the history books are incomplete. So much information was lost when the great library of Alexandria burned...' My voice faltered. From his expression, I could tell I hadn't told him that part.

There was a moment's silence. Then, 'Well, as long as you're feeling so helpful, what do you propose we do about Roxanne?'

I said a bad word.

'I already told you I wasn't going to touch her again,' he said smugly.

'Send her north with Craterus then,' I said.

'You still haven't forgiven her for trying to poison you?'

He could sound almost innocent when he wanted.

I rolled over and glared at him.

'Alexander, listen to me. I'm only going to say this once. I have not forgiven Roxanne for anything she's done. Poisoning me was just the last straw. Send her north with Craterus. It's not going to be like this much longer.' I heaved a huge sigh.

'Will you really try and save me?' he asked.

It was the same question every day. His eyes were sad sometimes, and sometimes they were hopeful. I smiled and traced the shape of his nose, the arched brows; his long lashes tickled my hands. 'I promise,' I told him, and I kissed him. Our kiss grew deeper and his hands roamed over my body.

He moved onto me like a wave breaking over the beach. 'Oh, Ashley,' he whispered, 'sometimes I feel as if my whole life was just a dream, and tomorrow I'll wake up and none of this will have ever happened.'

'What would you regret the most?' I asked. 'Beating Darius? Conquering all of Persia? Seeing India?'

'I would regret this the most,' he said, his breath catching in his throat as he moved on me, slowly sliding back and forth, letting his body speak for him. I would have thought he was happy, except for the tears falling on my shoulders.

Alexander had separated the army into three sections, sending Craterus and Seleucos northwards with the elephants and Roxanne. Nearchus took the navy and sailed along the coast. And we went into the Gedrosian desert. At first, the journey seemed easy. There was plenty of water, and game abounded. We were headed towards home, and the soldiers sang as they marched.

We had the hipparchies – archers on horseback – with us, almost all the cavalry, the rank and file, and a huge group made up of mostly soldiers' wives and children, and families that had hitched onto the army for the return trip. The front part of the army was marching easily along. At the back, the wagons full of civilians dragged sometimes several days' march behind. It didn't worry Alexander too much; his scouts made sure there was no threat to anyone. But he was uneasy, his handsome face sombre as he walked or rode at the head of his army.

The people in our tent, Brazza, Axiom, Usse, and Plexis had somehow picked up Alexander's melancholy mood. I think there were two reasons for it; he had not stopped thinking about what I'd said, and the strain of knowing he had less than two years to live was sapping his strength. He knew now he was marching towards his destiny in Babylon. Moreover, he was still bitterly disappointed that his soldiers hadn't wanted to continue with him further into India.

We had no privacy to talk, so he had to ruminate on every issue by himself. I wanted desperately to find time alone with him, but it was impossible on the first leg of our journey.

Our tent was swamped with people at night when we set up camp – and during the day, Alexander didn't have a single moment to himself. Even when he went to bathe there was always a petition to sign, a problem to settle, or someone to see him.

'Can it wait until I'm finished?' he asked peevishly as another man came into the tent with one more papyrus scroll to endorse. He poked his head around the screen that separated the chamber pot from the rest of the tent. 'I'll be out in a minute. Just wait outside, will you?'

The man looked abashed and left the tent. I heard a loud sigh from Alexander and a click as he rolled up the scroll he'd been reading on the toilet. 'I don't have time to do anything anymore,' he griped as he carried the pot outside and gave it to a slave to empty. After a cursory glance, he signed the scroll and came back in to help us.

Brazza and I got busy packing up the tent. We would be marching in less than an hour, and we were running late. Axiom took the fragile glass lamp and poured out the oil, then he carefully packed it in a box lined with sawdust to keep it from breaking.

I took the bedcovers off the bed and folded them away. They would need a good cleaning soon, next time we set up camp I would see to that. Our clothes were getting grubby too. I wrinkled my nose and plucked at the linen tunic I was wearing. It was a fine, herringbone weave, but it was getting smelly. I would have loved to find a Happy Travels Inn just over the next rise, but that chain of hotels wouldn't make it to the world before another two thousand five hundred years. I would have to put up with the tent and my dirty clothes for a while longer.

Chiron was in his playpen. It was a very useful thing, made of slender ash wood and easy to set up or put away. It had been made by one of the men in charge of fixing the long spears used in the phalanx. The broken spears were turned into the pen. Some of the bars had marks notched into them. I was afraid to ask what these notches represented. I was sure I knew what the answer would be.

When I finished the bedcovers, I put away Chiron's toys and got him ready to travel; packing his diapers and his food in my saddlebags. We would only stop marching when the sun set.

Alexander completed his affairs. He checked his armour, smoothed the leather straps and laid the bronze breastplate with its enamelled Gorgon's head in his gilded wooden chest. When everything was put away he turned to me, his eyes sad. 'I can't believe I'll never wear them again in battle,' he said with a deep sigh.

I shook my head. 'I can't believe you're saying that. I thought you were glad to stop fighting.'

He looked crestfallen. 'I said that?'

'You did. Axiom! I'm all set here.' I picked up Chiron out of his playpen and put him in Alexander's arms. 'We're going to start reading *The Odyssey* tonight, you promised.'

'I did, didn't I?' He sounded pleased. He loved reading. We'd just received *The Odyssey* in the mail. Alexander's mother, Olympias, had sent it nearly two years ago. Although I hated my mother-in-law for kidnapping my son Paul, I was glad to get a new book to read.

'We finished *The Iliad* months ago. Since then, we haven't read anything. Besides, I got to the point where I didn't like Achilles,' I said, braiding my hair and tying it with string.

'You what?'

'He was always sulking,' I explained, fastening my tunic tightly around my waist. 'I much preferred Hector. I cried when he died.'

'So did I, he was so brave. What was your favourite part?' Alexander loved talking about *The Iliad*. I liked it too, but I had gotten tired of all the bloodshed, described in gory detail by the blind poet.

'I think I liked the part when Hector's father Priam comes to see Achilles and he actually kisses his hand. I think that was the bravest thing anyone did in the whole story.' I was ready to go. I peeked out the tent and saw my horse being led up. 'But I tired of the men always telling the women to do the same thing, "Go back to your quarters and take care of your weaving. Go and give orders to the servants." How degrading! As if all they could do was weave or order slaves around!'

'Well, what else did you think they could do?' Alexander frowned. 'You don't think Hector was going to tell his wife, "Grab a spear and come and fight with me! I'm about to go and get killed fighting an immortal"? No! He had his son to think about and he wanted his wife to take care of the babe.'

'Bullshit. He knew he was going to be killed, and he knew his wife would be sold into slavery and his son would most likely be killed as well. He was just being your typical male. All brawn and no brains.'

'What would you have had him do?' Alexander looked scandalized. I was slandering one of his heroes.

'I don't know. Maybe pack up and leave in the dead of night.'

'You mean run away?' His voice rose several octaves and Axiom poked his head back in the tent to see if anyone had been stabbed.

'Yes, run away. What's the use of dying for a lost cause? He knew Troy was about to be burned to the ground and everyone in it killed or enslaved. If he really loved his wife and son, he would have done anything to save them including saving his own neck. Don't you think his father, Priam, would have liked to know that his son and grandson were safe somewhere?'

Alexander scratched his head. 'How long have you lived here, I mean in this time?'

'Ten years, I think.' I frowned. 'I suppose you're going to say something spiteful like, are all your people cowards?'

'No, but you didn't quite catch the mentality of the

heroes in the story. They thought it was better to die gloriously than to live in shame.'

'*Really*?' My voice was sarcastic. 'And I suppose you think the same? You would gallop off to war knowing you were about to be slaughtered and that I would end up in a silver mine somewhere, literally slaving away. And that Chiron would be killed.' My words caught in my throat.

'Oh, Ashley.' He tilted his head to the side and contemplated me. 'We're not talking about *The Iliad*, are we? You're talking about me and you.'

'And Chiron and Paul.' I tried to smile but it wobbled across my face. 'Alex, I couldn't bear to lose you. If Hector thought that he and his family could be saved, don't you think he'd have acted differently? Even if it meant giving up the fight and running away?'

'I don't think so.' Alexander sounded sad. '*The Iliad* was a tragedy. It was meant to make us think about the perfidy of the gods and men. In *The Iliad*, there's not much hope for anyone. Everyone is manipulated.' We were silent a minute, our eyes locked together. His expression finally made me lower mine. He still believed in fate.

'I know, but at least in *The Odyssey* the women do a bit more.' I sighed.

'Like what?'

'Well, they're always giving baths to the heroes in that story. I like the part where the handsome son of Ulysses takes off his ...'

'I think,' Alexander interrupted with a grin, 'your idea of action and mine are quite different.'

'I wouldn't say that,' I teased. Alexander helped me put

Chiron on the back of my pony and I checked to make sure that the waterskins were full. 'Will you walk with me?' I asked. I was glad to see him smiling and I wanted to pursue our conversation.

He shook his head. 'I'll see you this evening, and we'll start reading *The Odyssey* together. However, right now I have to go see Ptolemy Lagos. He wanted to tell me something important.'

'Oh?' I raised my eyebrows. 'What does he want to tell you?'

'If I knew, I wouldn't have to see him.' Alexander sounded exasperated. 'Go weave your wool, Woman, and give orders to your servants!'

'If I had been Hector's wife, I would have hit him over the head with my loom.' I said, sourly.

'Liar, you were crying when he bade her goodbye.' Alexander leaned over and kissed me, his eyes twinkling.

'Will you tell me what Ptolemy says?' I was curious.

Alexander shook his head. 'If I think you need to know.' He kissed me again, and I walked off leading my pony. Chiron was thrilled; he loved riding. To prove it he reached over and yanked one of my braids.

The land was rich in strange plants, and the botanists were perhaps the happiest people in the army at that point. As I walked along, I saw the scientists scrambling about picking leaves and roots and tucking them in their pouches. Even Usse was busy gathering the different types of plants. He was interested in anything that might be a new form of medicine.

My mould had been a success and now Usse was trying to grow even more of it. So far, he thought he'd saved three soldiers from certain death using the blue-green mould we'd grown on old bread. One of the men had cut his leg to the bone when he fell off his horse. The cut had festered and the leg had turned an angry red. Usse had packed the wound full of mouldy bread and a week later the man was still alive.

He wasn't completely well yet. This was not a shot of antibiotics. Nevertheless, the leg had ceased to swell and the redness had gone down. Slowly, healthy pink skin was taking over, so maybe we had something.

Late that afternoon we arrived in front of a vast forest of brambles. The bushes grew so close together and the thorns were so long and sharp that we ended up camping while the soldiers took turns hacking a passage through the impenetrable thickets.

I decided to find a place to wash while we were waiting. There was a large brook flowing nearby. I packed our dirty laundry on a pony, and put Chiron in his backpack. After walking upstream for half an hour I found the perfect spot. There was nobody in sight, I had found a deserted bend in the stream and the only thing that saw me was a large vulture circling very high above us in the empty sky. I looked at the big bird and frowned. Half the army would be saying it was a bad omen. The other half would be claiming it was a good omen. The East and the West were not uniting as smoothly as Alexander had hoped.

The stream wound around a sharp bend, splashed onto

a large rock, and swirled into a small deep pool. I hobbled the pony, bathed Chiron, then tied the little boy to a low tree so he couldn't crawl away. I washed everything including my own tunic and hung the wet laundry on thorn bushes to dry. Then I went swimming. It was heavenly. The water was dark green, nearly turquoise, and pollution hadn't been invented yet so I could even drink it. I hauled myself onto a warm rock and sat in the sun to dry.

Chiron and I napped in the shade of a thorn tree. When I woke up the sun had moved, so I went to check to see if the laundry had dried. I had just finished, when Alexander came galloping down the bank. The horse's hooves made a loud clatter on the rocky ground. He threw himself off the horse and tossed the reins over a branch. I wondered why he was in such a hurry; usually he hated to rush.

He didn't see me at first – I was sitting in the shade near Chiron, who was playing with some flat rocks, piling them up and knocking them down again. I waved 'Over here!'

'Ashley!' He limped hurriedly over to me.

I stood when I saw his face. 'What is it?'

'Ptolemy told me something incredible.' He ran a hand through his hair, making it stand up in wild curls. The skin on his face was drawn tight.

'What is going on?' I asked, worried now.

'It's Roxanne's doing. She sent someone to fetch Paul from the valley of Nysa. Ptolemy told me that he's being brought to Babylon.'

'But, why?' I sat down slowly, my legs felt weak.

'My mother must have ordered her to do that. She

11

never would have thought of it herself.'

I turned a frozen face up towards my husband. 'Or it could be Stateira's orders. She's ruling Babylon. She means to kill him, doesn't she?'

'I don't know!' he cried. Then seeing my expression, he shook his head. 'No, Stateira wouldn't dare touch him, and I think Roxanne has no evil intent. She simply followed Olympias's orders.'

'When did Ptolemy find out about this?' My voice shook.

'I think he's known for some time. But he didn't dare tell me.'

'Did you tell him you knew he was sleeping with Roxanne?' I asked.

'Of course. At first, he thought I was going to kill him. He knelt in front of me and said he would understand.'

I laughed mirthlessly. 'He did? What happens now?'

'We send messages. The boy will be safe, I think, and we'll see him when we arrive in Babylon.'

'Who will take care of him until then? Will Roxanne get to him first, or will we?'

'Ptolemy said he was to be sent to Babylon, that's all he overheard.'

'Who exactly did he overhear?'

'Roxanne and one of her priests. The man she sent to fetch him is a priest of the temple of Apollo. To make sure that they would get the boy they also sent a priestess from the temple of Artemis.'

'The cold and merciless goddess,' I said, shivering.

'Nobody will dare harm him; he's protected by the

moon herself. Don't worry. We'll find him in Babylon.'

'Sharwah won't let him leave the valley. Maybe we don't have to worry.'

Alexander pulled me to my feet and drew me close to him. 'He will have to let him go. Roxanne used the royal seal on the order. Lysimachus gave it to her. He thought he was doing me a favour. He couldn't understand why I never tried to see Roxanne. I have to tell you something else Ptolemy told me. Lysimachus is sharing her bed now. I'm sure that's what made Ptolemy talk.'

'Lysimachus gave Roxanne the royal seal? How could he *do* such a thing?' I shivered and looked over Alexander's shoulder, as if I could see past the thousand miles that separated us from the valley of Nysa. 'How long will it take for Paul to arrive in Babylon?'

'I'm not sure, it depends on the passes and the weather,' said Alexander.

'And when will we arrive?'

'I have no idea,' he admitted.

'Great.' I nearly kept the sarcasm out of my voice.

Alexander blushed. He looked down at his feet and frowned. Finally he said, 'I don't know what to say, Ashley. I thought he would be safe there. I never would have believed Roxanne capable of doing something like this. I feel as helpless as you do. I'm sorry.' He looked up at me, his eyes pained.

I was furious, but I couldn't hold him responsible. He had sworn not to touch Roxanne, and she was just paying him back for all the slights, real or imaginary, she blamed on him, starting with the death of her child. His child. I put

13

my hand on his arm and gave him a little squeeze. 'And I'm sorry too. I keep forgetting that he was your son. It must have hurt you very much.'

Alexander looked down at Chiron. 'I never told her how sorry I was. Do you think I was unkind?'

'At the time we thought she murdered the babe,' I reminded him.

'I still do,' he said. 'Now I worry about Paul.'

'Do you remember what Sharwah said about him being protected by the moon? I do believe he is protected by something.' I tried to sound brave.

Alexander nodded but didn't smile. 'I hate being so far away.'

'I do too,' I said bleakly. I gathered up the washing and put it on the pony's back. 'As long as you're here you might as well help. Can you take Chiron?' I put my tunic on and untied his horse.

I led the horses while Alexander carried Chiron. We were silent as we picked our way across the stony ground. I had never wanted to leave my son, Paul. Now he was in danger again, and there was nothing I could do; there were no aeroplanes, trains, telephones, or police officers to call. All we could do was send messages by horse and by carrier pigeon, and pray that they arrive in time to save the life of our first-born son. Until we got to Babylon, we had lots of time to wait and to dread. Babylon, where everything would be decided. Babylon, where I hoped to find our son alive, and where Alexander was to die.

Although the land we were travelling through was arid,

it was full of life. It was also treacherous in ways we did not expect. We'd been marching for three weeks, and everyone was tired. Alexander had been looking for a likely spot to set up camp in order to let the stragglers catch up and to organize the army. We were approaching deep sand and the wagons had to be lightened. So he and the generals decided to bivouac in a long wide valley.

We entered the valley and the army camped on one side of a sloping plateau, high above the riverbed. Thousands of tents were set up in straight lines. Then the supply tents, smithy tents, and cooks set up shop around them. The horses were corralled downstream from us, but also on a plateau. Thick woods grew on the far side of the valley opposite the encampment. When the civilians started to arrive with their wagons, sometimes days after the army, the only place left to camp was in the valley bottom, along the banks of the stream.

The stream was shallow, though wide, and some soldiers immediately set about building a bathhouse. Other soldiers went into the woods to gather firewood. Priests began making sacrifices to the various gods, and the cooks heated their clay pots to bake bread.

I was glad to be travelling with the head of the army. Axiom had chosen a tranquil spot not far from the stream. We were near the kitchen tents, and the cooks spoiled Chiron, saving little treats for him when they fixed the rations. Today someone had found a plover's nest and presented the eggs to me.

I thanked the man who'd brought me the eggs, wishing I had Alexander's formidable memory for names. Since there were at least two hundred cooks travelling with us, I suppose I could be forgiven for not knowing all of them. Then I went outside and watched the shepherds milking the goats. Chiron would have fresh milk for dinner and hard-boiled eggs.

I sniffed the air and looked towards the horizon. In the desert, the air is so dry that a rainstorm can be smelled before it's seen. I smelled rain, but the sky was still clear except for a violet smudge near the faraway mountains. The storm was passing to the north.

That evening we read some of *The Odyssey*, and we got to the part where Hermes goes to see Calypso and tells her she must give up her lover, Ulysses. Alexander was reading. He had the best reading voice. When he got to that part, he faltered though. He looked at me and shivered.

I glanced at Plexis, who was sitting on his pallet, listening quietly. 'What do you think about that?' I asked.

His face was paler than normal and he spoke slowly. 'I think that Calypso is right; the gods are jealous. They guard their women.'

'But it sounds as if their women don't *want* to be guarded,' I said, 'Listen to what Calypso is saying!' I leaned over Alexander's shoulder and read, '"When Eos of the rosy fingertips fell in love with Orion, you gods were so jealous that you sent the chaste and merciless Artemis to kill him. Then, when fair-haired Demeter gave her heart to Jason, and in a newly ploughed field gave her body to him three times, Zeus was so jealous he killed Jason with a brilliant lightning bolt. Now the gods begrudge me my lover? I saved this man when he shipwrecked, alone on his boat after Zeus capsized and destroyed his vessel as it sailed upon the wine-dark sea. I saved him and promised to make him immortal, for ever young …"—'

I broke off and peered at Plexis. 'Does that sound like she wants to be guarded? It sounds like she wants to be left alone with her lover.'

'I think she should listen to Hermes and let him go,' said Plexis. 'Zeus's ire is to be feared above all things.'

'What form does his ire take?' I teased gently.

However, Plexis was serious. His eyes were wide as he looked across the tent at me. 'I would brave the anger of Zeus for you, my lady, but at least I know what I risk. I will tell you this; his anger is like a great storm that washes over everything. His lightning bolts are deadly weapons and the rain he sends can wash away the world.'

I flushed. I didn't like it when the conversation turned towards the gods. For one thing, talk about them made me uneasy. Plexis was sure they existed. For him, like in the stories, they were omnipresent, in every stream and tree, and always ready to make life difficult for us mortals. 'Can we read some more?' I asked. 'Please? I won't interrupt, and I won't take sides anymore.'

'Take sides?' Alexander turned towards me, a curious look on his face.

'Well, I won't say that Zeus has no business killing the goddess's lovers.'

'You can say that if you want to,' said Plexis. 'As a matter of fact, I'm hoping you will insist on that point.'

'You don't still think I'm a goddess?' I said crossly.

17

'Because if you're going to go scaring the cooks again …'

'I'm sorry about that,' chuckled Plexis. He loved playing jokes, but sometimes he went too far. He knew I was trying to wean Chiron so he'd gone to see the cooks and I had been presented with thirty-five, pure white nanny goats. Milk goats, all of them. They had been tied outside the tent and they'd baa'd all night long, making any sleep impossible. I'd managed to get rid of the goats, giving them back to the shepherds. However, the cooks hadn't stopped and this evening an enormous pot of honey had been found outside the tent-flap. I had Plexis carry it back – we couldn't eat it all, and I wanted the soldiers to be able to have a treat. Honey was the only sweetener known at that time and the cooks made honey-cakes and honeyed almonds with it.

'I don't think you're a goddess,' said Plexis, 'But do you think maybe the gods think you are?'

'They don't.' I lay back on the bed. 'Can you read some more, Alexander?'

'No, I'm tired.' Alexander passed me the story. 'Maybe Axiom will read.'

However, Axiom shook his head and yawned. He was tired too. Brazza was a deaf-mute, he couldn't read aloud, and Plexis had a sore throat from yelling at the cavalry all day long. I couldn't read aloud very well at all. Ancient Greek was lacking in punctuation and all the words were stuck together. I would run out of breath and then break off at the wrong point, destroying the careful rhythm and beauty of the poem. I sighed and carefully rolled up the precious scroll, wondering how Ulysses was going to get off the island where he'd been shipwrecked.

Next morning, I took all the bedding outside. Axiom, Brazza, and I washed it. It wasn't a very interesting day, except, for some reason, I decided I didn't like where the tent was set up and decided to move it.

It took us all morning, but we moved everything to a little hill overlooking the encampment. It was the first time I'd ever made a decision like that. Normally Axiom picked out the place where the tent would be, but he didn't say anything. He just sighed when I showed him where I wanted to move.

Once up on the hill, I felt much better. The reason I wanted to move may have been the crowding. Usually our tent was isolated. However, the families following the army were camped down by the riverside, and more and more people were arriving. Soon the valley was packed solid with tents and wagons. It was noisy, and I was glad to be away from the bustle.

Then I decided I wanted to take a real bath, so I gave Chiron to Brazza and went to inspect the new sauna. It was just how I liked it. A large bathtub in one corner, a pile of steaming rocks, a cauldron of hot water, a bucket of soft clay soap, and twenty-five naked soldiers.

I washed my hair, admired the scenery, and gave my traditional blessing in English. *'Great bodies, guys, keep up the good work.'*

Afterwards, I went to the mess tent and spoke to some Egyptian cooks. They were busy making beer, their favourite drink. The Greeks preferred wine and the

Persians preferred cooked wine that resembled mead. The cooks had a friendly rivalry among them. The Egyptians made the best bread, the Persians made delicious meat dishes, and the Greeks had the nicest goat cheese. Since we'd been to India, the cooks had stocked up on tons of spices. Now the whole camp smelled like curry. Before, the strongest smell had been garlic. Now, it could be cardamom, cinnamon, curry, or even mint, depending on the menu. Today it was curry, and I noticed most of the goats were missing.

I took a wineskin and filled it with fresh beer. The cooks gave me a honey-cake for Chiron. I thanked them and wandered back to the tent. The air was shimmering with heat. My nerves were tingling. I looked up at the sky and frowned. The smell of rain was very sharp but, as before, there was only the faintest smudge of dark clouds on the horizon. I was sure it would rain and decided to gather up all the bedclothes before they were ruined.

The blankets were still damp, but I insisted. Axiom sighed again – I was being unreasonable that day – and he set up the clothes line inside the tent. I was nervous for some reason. I could always tell when a storm was coming. The electricity in the air was making goose bumps on my arms. Even Chiron was cranky, although the honey-cake calmed him down quickly.

We ate dinner in the tent. It was spicy curried goat and Egyptian beer. Plexis and Alexander took turns reading from *The Odyssey*. We were right at the part where Ulysses was in the midst of a raging storm at sea. His raft had been smashed to pieces but luckily, a sea-nymph gave him a magic scarf to wrap around his chest. Sort of like a life jacket, I decided. He was about to be smashed against the cliffs by a giant wave, when Athena, the goddess with the parti-coloured eyes, saved him. At that moment, a huge clap of thunder shook the tent and we all jumped.

We stared uneasily at each other. The lamp swung giddily as a gust of wind and rain swept into the tent. Plexis leapt up and fastened the tent flap, while Axiom made sure that the tent pole was secured. Brazza picked up Chiron, who was wailing with fright, and Alexander bent his head back down to the story, intending to read on. However, thunder continued to boom and his words were lost in the storm. He shrugged, rolled the parchment up carefully, and put it in the box at the foot of the bed. Plexis got his out mending, and Axiom and I sorted through the bedcovers, putting the dry ones on the beds and shaking the damp ones out and hanging them up again.

Brazza played with Chiron until the little boy dropped off to sleep, then he put him in his hammock. I curled up next to Alexander and he rubbed my back and tickled my neck. Driving rain and howling wind lasted nearly an hour. The storm passed by, moving towards the hills. Axiom blew out the lamp and I yawned sleepily. Tomorrow I was planning on taking a ride; I hadn't ridden Lenae in a week. I could take a picnic and maybe Plexis could come with me. I lay in bed planning what I would take: a jug of beer, a loaf of freshly baked Egyptian bread with cardamom seeds, soft goat's cheese with honey, an apple, some cold curried goat, a handful of raisins...sleep claimed me before I could finish my picnic.

That night there was a flash flood. A solid wall of muddy water crashed into the encampment, sweeping away tents, people, livestock, and wagons full of supplies. We were very lucky. I had insisted on camping on a small rise, so we were spared, but the families that followed the army were less fortunate. They had camped by the stream, and in ten minutes thousands of people were swept away with their belongings. It was a terrible loss. More people died in that one flood than in Alexander's worst battle.

The noise was like a freight train crashing into the camp. We were catapulted out of our beds by the roar. It was worse than anything I'd ever heard before. Screams and cries followed it, and then an eerie silence. Chiron started wailing.

Alexander leapt out of bed and crashed into Plexis, both men yelled as they hit the floor. Axiom jumped up and quickly lit the lamp while Brazza, who'd felt the vibration of the noise, groped for a torch. We piled out of the tent, torches held high, and stared into the darkness.

Low clouds blocked the moonlight and there were no stars. The blackness was lit by torches as soldiers rushed about. Flickering lights reflected off the white water in the gorge. Instead of a shallow stream, there was now a raging torrent. We stared in horror at the devastation. Nearly half the civilian camp had disappeared. Where camp fires and torches normally dotted the ground, there was nothing but swift churning water, and empty darkness instead of a sleeping camp.

We slept no more. Soldiers rushed downstream, frantically searching for survivors. I walked along the banks of the river, my torch held in shaking hands, and pulled everything I could find out of the water.

I found rugs, branches, tent-poles, tunics, a wooden doll, three nearly drowned children, a drowned woman, and a live camel that bit me.

The three children were carried to the infirmary by soldiers who'd come running at my cries. The drowned woman was impaled on a tent pole and I couldn't pull her off. I screamed and some soldiers came to help me. The camel was thrashing in the shallows, its legs tangled in a bush. I tried to put a rope around its neck and the damn beast bit my arm. I left it, sure it would be all right.

Further downstream, the flood had piled hundreds of tents upon each other. We saved only five people from that mess. Nearly five hundred perished on the river bend. The tents were heavy with water and the people inside them were drowned or smothered. After a few hours of helping the soldiers trying to find survivors, I was so deeply in shock I thought couldn't feel anymore.

I pulled a sodden rug off a child's body and choked back a scream. The little girl was still clutching her doll. Her face was streaked with mud and I gently wiped it away. Then I picked her up and carried her to the long line of bodies lying on the ground. But there I was stuck. I didn't want to put her down. I couldn't put her down with the other bodies. I honestly don't know what I was thinking, but I couldn't let go. All I could do was stand there and sob. One of the soldiers ran to get Usse when I refused to let go of the child. He gently took her from my arms and led me back to our tent.

The sound of graves being dug and rocks being piled to form cairns lasted for days. I sat in the tent and tried to shut out the noise, but there was no way to do so. After a week we left, leaving behind us nearly five thousand graves of men, women, and children.

The army was stunned. We walked with our heads bowed and tears on our cheeks. The sobs and laments of the men and women who'd lost everything followed us. They had lost their families, their belongings, and their animals. Alexander promised everyone that they would never want as long as they followed him. He swore to replace their belongings, but their families would lie for ever beneath the rocky ground in Gedrosia.

We reached an oasis and camped for another week, getting our bearings and letting the shock wear off. I'd been a wreck since the flood, clutching Chiron to my breast, thanking the gods over and over that we'd camped on the rise.

We felt better after a few days in the oasis, but our troubles were just beginning. Instead of following the setting sun, Alexander decided to turn south, towards the sea. He was worried that Nearchus wouldn't be able to replenish supplies for his navy, so he wanted to rendezvous with him at the coast.

For nearly two days, we trekked through parched land to the sea, but there we found no sign of Nearchus.

Getting increasingly anxious, Alexander hugged the coast as we walked further and further into the desert. By now, it was too late to turn back. We had no more water;

our only choice was to continue and hope that the guides could find the wells they promised us.

We walked in single file. The chariots and wagons bogged down in the deep sand, and the horses struggled and floundered. Little by little the army shed its extra weight. Wagons were left behind. Anything that couldn't be carried was dropped into the burning sand and forgotten. The army didn't suffer, but the families that followed us were sorely tried. Those who survived the flood lost their remaining belongings to the sand.

Alexander walked at the head of his army. His skin became burnt and his hair was bleached white-blond by the sun. He wrapped his cloak around him and struggled onwards. After three days of roasting in the hot oven of the desert, he knew that he had to change tactics or we would never make it through. We set the tents up during the day and stayed in their shade, waiting for evening. Everyone slept if they could or just sat and sweltered if they couldn't.

Then the guides told him that they were lost, which was the cruellest blow of all.

Actually *we* weren't lost, the springs and wells were. We arrived at one only to find it full of shifting sand. It took a whole day for the Arabs who were with us to dig it out and find a pittance of water for the parched army. The landmarks were scarce. The guides were not sure where the next oasis was.

For the traveller lost in the desert the best advice is to hide in the shade during the day, moving as little as possible and then march at night, so that's what we did for nearly a month. The whole army moved at night, following the torches planted in the deep sand by the scouts. We moved in single file because the sand got heavier and harder and harder to walk in. I walked; leading my mare with Chiron tied to her back. Brazza walked behind me, and Axiom walked just behind Brazza. I think Alexander was afraid I'd fall asleep as I walked. I never did though. I walked through the quiet dark, keeping my eyes on the flickering orange light of the torches, with one hand on Chiron's leg to make sure he was still there. No one spoke. The air was parched and we saved what little moisture we had in our throats and mouths. Everyone wrapped linen scarves over their faces. Silently we walked through the night. The only noise was the soft swish, swish of dry sand under our feet. The worst thing about the night marches was the fact that you *could* fall asleep while walking. Some men did, and woke up when the burning sun was too hot to bear. Then they would try to follow the army's trail under the inferno of the desert sky. Hardly anyone ever caught up.

The deep sand and the desiccated landscape claimed the horses. Plexis was nearly hysterical with grief. He lost over half of his hipparchie. Only the strongest animals survived. The camels did much better than the horses. Luckily, all the elephants had been sent with Craterus. Poor Plexis, the desert journey was a nightmare from start to finish for him.

After one particularly harrowing march over salt flats where the hard crust supported a man's weight but broke under the horses' hooves causing the poor beasts to flounder and thrash for miles, some dying of exhaustion, some from the heat, Plexis came to the tent. He'd been up all night with the horses. He was covered with salt and sand. Tears made silver trails down his dusty cheeks. He staggered and fell to his knees.

'I can't go on,' he said hoarsely. 'They're all dying, all of them. There's just enough water for my men; the horses are dying of thirst out there ...' he broke off and sobbed.

Alexander moved across the tent and crouched by his friend. He had just been speaking to a guide, and there was reported to be a desert spring not far ahead, if we could just hang on one more day.

'Plexis, tomorrow night we'll have water, I promise.' Alexander's voice was harsh; the salt and sand irritated our throats.

Plexis raised his head. He seemed to see us for the first time. I was sitting cross-legged, nursing Chiron. With the water shortage, the little boy was nursing more frequently which was good for him, less so for me. I was nearly out of my mind with thirst. His eyes settled on Chiron and he held out his arms.

Chiron was walking now. He toddled happily over to his father, his face the only one of ours with a smile. 'Papa!' he cried.

There was a moment's stunned silence, then Plexis said, 'What, what did you say?' He rocked back on his heels, a mixture of pride and fear on his face.

We all gaped. Chiron babbled all the time, but he had yet to say a real word. 'Papa,' he said quite clearly, and he tripped on a bump in the rug and fell into Plexis's arms.

'He said "Papa", did you hear that? He said "Papa"!' Plexis looked around, his face split in a huge grin.

I buried my head in Alexander's chest.

'What's the matter?' His arms came around me, holding me tight.

'I don't know,' I whispered into Alexander's ear. 'I'm so tired, and so happy. I wanted to see Plexis smile for the longest time, he's been so terribly sad lately.'

He nodded, his chin on my shoulder, and tightened his arms around me.

Plexis watched us, an uncertain smile on his lips. 'What's going to happen now?' he asked softly.

'I wish I knew,' I said unhappily.

After marching all night long we reached the spring. We stayed as long as possible, replenishing our water supply and sending scouts to plan the next stage of the journey. The spring was a very large one, nearly an oasis, with date palms and even a meagre pasture for the horses. After everyone had drunk and filled the canteens, I filled a bathtub and soaked in it. I sat in the tub all day long, Chiron slept on my chest, his legs in the water, his head on my shoulder, blissfully cool for the first time in weeks.

The next day we set off again, the heat assailed us once more, and men and horses suffered.

There's a story about Alexander, marching through the desert in the blistering heat, with everyone practically dying of thirst around him, pouring a helmet full of water out on the sand rather than drinking it all by himself. It is a noble story, and I'm sure Alexander would have done such a thing had a scout ever brought back a helmet full of water as proof that a spring lay ahead. He would never have drunk water if his men could not. He would be the first to die of thirst. He was always the last to drink when we reached a spring. However, the men didn't die of thirst in that desert, the horses did. The men died because they fell asleep during the night marches and they panicked the next day, rushing under the blazing sun to catch up.

I'll never know where the tale about the water came from. Especially, as I've said, we mostly marched at night. Nevertheless, I always liked that story. It does capture the 'Spirit of Alexander', I think.

# Chapter Two

One morning we arrived at a very strange place. We found it by the smell. After marching for days through a lunar desert, where strange, free-form rocks reared up from white sand that looked like powdered sugar, we reached the coast once more. Instead of the clean, sharp smell of salt water, there was a strong, almost overpowering odour of dead fish.

There, perched on cliffs, was a scarecrow village. The men and women who lived there were small and frail, and strange to look upon. They had wide mouths, pale, globular eyes, and skin that had been burnt brown by the unrelenting sun. The children were silent as they came to meet us. Children had always been the first to rush out to see the army, running alongside the soldiers, shouting and laughing. Except these children, who stood without speaking, their fingers in their mouths, their eyes flat and staring. It gave us the shivers. The men and women were not any more talkative. There reigned an unnatural silence in that village.

Alexander inquired after his navy and learned, to his relief, that they had stopped there not six days earlier, and had left after stocking up on fresh water and fish. For the place we had come to was a fishing village. The miserable huts were made of straw and shells. Hundreds of little fishing boats were just arriving in the harbour; they fished all night, coming to land during the day. Huge piles of pure white salt lay around the village, and I soon found out why the huts were made of straw.

All the wood gleaned in the nearby hills and found washed up on the beach went towards making crates. The fish were cleaned, salted, and packed in crates to be trekked by donkey caravan towards the cities.

We stayed for two days, camped near this austere little village, to the great wonderment of the fisherman. They had already seen the great fleet of Nearchus, and now they witnessed Alexander's army. It would make for many long conversations while they fished, salted and walked their scrawny donkeys down the trails. At least, I hoped so; of all the places I'd seen, this was the most desolate. Even the water here wasn't completely free of salt. The wells were lined with shells to keep the sand out, but the salt and smell of rotting fish pervaded everything.

We left, following the narrow path the fish-eaters took on their way to the city of Bampur. At least now, there was a path to follow. We headed along the coast towards the setting sun.

The next two weeks is a blur in my memory. Each day's march resembled the one before it. We were silent, walking through the hostile landscape along the white path before us. Birds wheeled overhead and gazelles would sometimes be seen from a great distance. Slowly the desert gave away to scrub brush and sand was replaced by rocks, then wiry grass. I saw snakes and lizards, gerbils, and a mongoose. I liked seeing the animals, they broke the monotony of the walk, and it meant we were slowly approaching the Bampur valley.

We had two weeks of marching through arid land before we came to Bampur. The most difficult part of our journey was over.

We'd lost more than five thousand souls in the desert. We arrived exhausted, our clothes in tatters, and deeply shocked by all the men, women, and children who'd perished. We were relieved to be in a place where sweet water flowed in abundance and the grass grew green. It was like a rebirth, like arriving in paradise, and to top everything off, the whole city had turned out to greet Alexander, conquering hero and king of the world.

*Alexander, conquering hero!* People lined the streets. They were on the rooftops, and they were already hoarse from cheering by the time we were near enough to hear them.

*Alexander, king of the world!* Flowers fell like rain, wine flowed like rivers, the soldiers were fêted and acclaimed and Alexander's name was on everyone's lips. He had returned to his kingdom and the city, like a bride, opened her arms to him.

It was heady stuff for a man suddenly to realize that this was the summit of his glory. He had been fighting for so long that he'd forgotten why. He'd been struggling to reclaim a crown and consolidate a kingdom and now that it was done, suddenly, here it was. Here was his kingdom. It was just the edge, but it was here, and the people were weeping, screaming, and swooning when they saw him.

Even I, who had seen one of the ancient newsreels of

the Beatles arriving in America, was very impressed. The Beatles were nothing compared to Alexander. These people had no social media holograms, and they had been waiting for months for a glimpse of the young king.

*Here he was!* And, by the gods, he was young! He was handsome! He waved and grinned and cried. His hair was bleached pale gold, his body burned deep brown, his eyes glittered blue and brown, and they were huge in his starving face. His purple cape was in tatters, but the mayor of the city gave him a new one. He wore the crown of Darius on his noble head and he carried the spear of a cavalry officer. His men had polished their bronze weapons until they shone in the red setting sun like drops of blood. The horses, wild with the scent of grass and water, whinnied and screamed at the crowds, and the crowds screamed back.

Everyone cried, everyone laughed. It was our first homecoming and we were drunk within seconds with the ecstasy of *nostos*, the epic return. We drank from the cups held out by every hand towards us. The men all had purple mouths and staggered drunkenly by the time we left the city and headed towards the encampment, but Alexander was drunk on glory. His eyes were exultant and his colour hectic. His face burned with fever and he had no voice left to speak.

We set up the tent and collapsed. The city revelled without us. Everyone in the army slept for the first night. Faintly in the distance I heard the sounds of the fête that was to last nearly a week, the whole time we were there. However, the sounds soon faded as I slid towards sleep wrapped in the arms of my hero, Alexander.

We both awoke early the next morning. Axiom had risen and was making a fire. Alexander and I looked at each other and we both smiled. Then we touched our heads together and my hair slid off my shoulder in a silver shower. 'Are you happy?' I asked him.

'Right now I am.' He rolled onto his back, pulling me on top of him and nuzzling my neck.

I kept rolling, giggling as I pulled him on top of me.

'Oh? Like that huh?' He grinned. His eyes darkened. 'It has been too long,' he said then, urgently. 'By the gods, it's been too long. I can't wait.' He shuddered once, twice, and groaned loudly. His body slumped, his cheek resting on mine.

I ran my hands down his back, wincing at his thinness, at how his hipbones met mine with a knock that could practically be heard. I grinned ruefully. We were like two scarecrows. 'Don't worry about it,' I whispered. 'What we need isn't love, we have enough of that. What we need are some good meals and rest. We'll see how you do in a week.'

'A week?' He raised his head and lifted an elegant eyebrow. 'Give me five minutes, I'll show you something.'

I chuckled. 'You will huh? I think I'll take you up on that.' There was something irresistible about being in bed, under the covers, naked with him.

He was right, in five minutes he showed me.

'Was that better?' he gasped, when he'd got his breath back.

'Mmm, I'll tell you in a minute,' I said lazily.

'A minute? Why not now?' he asked.

'Because I want to sleep, like *you* usually do. Why aren't you sleeping? Alex? Alex?'

I leaned over. His lashes were absurdly long when his eyes were closed.

That afternoon I spent an hour in the new bathhouse. I felt like a flower that had gone through a drought and was just feeling the spring rain falling. I slid into the hot water and closed my eyes; sheer bliss.

The bathhouse, my favourite place for the obvious reasons, was empty today. Everyone was recuperating or resting and the soldiers had strict orders to see to their equipment and their horses first before looking after themselves.

This was why we didn't see Plexis for two days. He had suffered terribly from the desert march. Each horse that fell was like a lost child for him and for Pharnabazus, the barbarian chieftain who had given us many of these horses and had accompanied us since the Caspian Sea. Together they'd managed to salvage most of the cavalry though. Now they had to be careful the horses didn't eat and drink themselves to death. The cavalry officers had to hobble and muzzle their horses around the clock, only letting them eat and drink for minutes at a time, so that they didn't get sick from drinking too fast or eating too much green grass.

Two days later the horses were turned out into a large pasture and Plexis tottered into the tent and passed out.

I was frightened. While Alexander was often on the verge of collapse because he didn't know when to stop,

Plexis had always been careful to save his strength. Now he lay on the floor of the tent. His eyes were open, staring, his hands were curled on his chest, and his forehead was burning hot.

I touched him and then raced out of the tent, crying for Usse. I was terrified. Plexis hadn't recognized me when I'd spoken his name. He had a fever that lasted for days. We kept him in bed and sponged his body with cool water, begging him to drink, but he didn't know us. He didn't seem to understand what we were saying. He tossed and turned as if he were possessed. Alexander sat by his bed until he was nodding with sleep then I would take his place. We relayed, with Axiom, Usse and Brazza, everyone putting cool cloths on his head, soothing his cries and trying to calm his fever. Finally he opened his eyes and recognized us. He forced a grin then sighed and slept. He slept for another twenty-four hours but his fever was gone. When he woke up he was ravenously hungry and devoured all Axiom's lentil stew.

We spoiled him all week, catering to him, bathing him, singing to him – except Alexander, thank the gods – and generally cheering him up. He liked it for about three days, then he started feeling a bit silly – no proper Athenian would ever admit to a little weakness – and soon he was up and around, playing with Chiron and back with his beloved horses. Everyone was euphoric; we were almost home and things were getting back to normal.

Well, almost normal.

One thing we'd all forgotten. It hadn't been so flagrant during the battles and the long journey – the Persians thought their king was a god. As a result, for the major part of Alexander's new kingdom *he was* a god. A real god, the one who makes the seasons change, the crops grow, and the sun rise. He was a divinity, in other words a very, very important VIP.

Alexander started to see what I'd been trying to tell him. The people of Persia expected him to be a new Darius, to join the line of rulers before him who had been divine. He was expected to hide behind a curtain, to wear Persian robes, to have people kneel and kiss the ground before him, and to be acclaimed as the representation of their god.

The Persian soldiers were thrilled; this was what they had been fighting for during the past ten years. The Greeks and the Macedonians were shocked. They had independent cities ruled by governors, and their king was a head of state, a figurehead in name only, like Alexander's father Philip had been. They were suddenly frightened that their independence was threatened.

The Egyptians said very little. They believed that Alexander was truly the son of Amon, and so they were content to wait and see what Alexander wanted. Meanwhile they prostrated themselves with the same fervour as the Persians, which shocked and angered the Greeks.

Strains and tensions started partitioning the army. A real schism was starting. Alexander was helpless to stop this. He had to hold so many different peoples together - it was the eternal story of trying to please everyone and pleasing no one. However, this deep split would divide his kingdom in half. We didn't feel it so much in Bampur; the differences were just beginning and things weren't so bad yet. The army was on its way home, and the only complaints came from the Greeks. Since they'd been griping for ten years, no one paid them any attention.

We travelled to the coast to meet Nearchus. Alexander had replenished his food and water stores, the army had recuperated well, Plexis said the horses were fit to move on, so on we went.

We were marching at the head of the army now, Alexander and I, leading Chiron on the back of my mare Lenaia, who had survived the terrible desert. The sun was setting but we didn't want to stop.

We could see the sea, a bright gold flash between black hills. We wanted to see how many of the ships had survived. After losing so many men, Alexander was terrified about his navy. To him the sea voyage must have been even worse, with no supplies or fresh water. We picked up the pace. Alexander was muttering to himself, a sure sign he was nervous. Suddenly a man stood up. He had been sitting on a rock, watching us as we drew nearer.

'Greetings, my good man,' said Alexander, friendly as usual. 'Is it far to the harbour from here? Would you know of a good place for my men to rest?'

'Do you not know me?' The voice was familiar, the figure, gaunt and dressed in tatters, was not.

Alexander stopped as if he'd been shot. His breath whistled out of his throat and his eyes suddenly filled with tears. 'Nearchus!' he cried, and threw himself into the man's arms.

'Nearchus?' I gasped. The admiral was long-haired, he had a beard, and his skin was burnt and peeling. I clapped my hands over my mouth, horrified.

The two men clasped each other's arms, tears sparkling on their faces. In the rays of the setting sun they were like black Chinese cut-outs capering in the middle of the dusty road, the golden sea glittering brightly behind them.

Alexander stopped and took Nearchus's face in his hands. 'What happened?' he asked, fear making his voice tremble. 'Has the navy been destroyed? How did you live? By the gods, Nearchus, I'm so glad to see you,' he broke off with a sob and kissed his friend hard on the mouth.

Nearchus shook his head; he was nearly laughing now. 'No, not at all, I'm fine. The voyage was difficult, to be sure, but the fleet is intact. We lost no boats and we lost but two men. Everyone is here. We are ready to sail. Come to the bay, you shall see.'

We fêted the navy for another week. The men had accomplished an amazing feat of exploration. Nearchus had managed to find fresh water and enough food to keep everyone alive. He told stories of great fish as long as the biggest boats and of colourful snakes that swam around the boats and terrorized the sailors. He claimed to have seen the sirens that were like woman with tails and the strange, dark seals that swim in the Arabian Sea.

'Did you really see a mermaid?' I asked Nearchus.

'I did,' he said. 'She was far away, and I saw but her profile. She waved and dived under the waves. She also cried something, before she disappeared under the water. She called out, 'Great Alexander lives! And still rules!'

That's how I knew you'd made it through the desert,' he told Alexander.

I was astounded. Nearchus, the most solid, unimaginative of men, had seen a mermaid? Well, why not? I cupped my hand on my chin and blinked at the red firelight while his voice droned on, telling of all the wonders he'd seen on the wide ocean. The 'Outer Sea', as he called it, to distinguish it from the 'Inner Sea' which was the Mediterranean.

I was sitting next to Plexis. The march had tired me out. I laid my head on his lap and fell asleep while he stroked my hair. I felt at peace.

But some people looked at me sleeping on Plexis's lap and frowned. Already the mantle of the king was subtly taking over that of the war-leader's armour. A king was not a captain. Alexander would be expected to place himself above all men. I would be expected to shut myself in the gynaeceum. No man could look upon the wife of a king. Plexis was actually touching me. In Persia, he would be instantly put to death.

Strange tensions wove into my dreams as I lay on my lover's lap. It didn't help any when Chiron woke up and toddled into the wide circle of men, looking for me. He saw Plexis and smiled. 'Papa!' he said proudly. It was still his only word and he used it for all the men in our tent. But now the men looked at the child with the triangular face, so like Plexis's, and his clear, hazel eyes, and they murmured between themselves. Alexander was deep in conversation with Nearchus but, even if he'd been watching carefully, he wouldn't have picked up the quick, flickering looks that were exchanged between his men. In some ways, he was an innocent.

# Chapter Three

The army packed up and moved on after a week, and the navy continued along the coast. Nearchus was heading towards Babylon, we were going to Suze. Before he left though, Alexander asked Nearchus to look for Paul. We still had no idea when he would arrive in Babylon. Nearchus said he would protect him with his life, and I felt much better. Nearchus could be trusted.

We celebrated Chiron's second birthday. Two years old already! He was a deceptively fragile-looking child, with fine bones and eyes that took up most of his face. But his eyes were full of bright intelligence and he had started talking. After Papa, he added Cala, for Kalanos, Brazza was Baza, and Axiom was Ax. I was 'Mummy', and he called Alexander 'Dada'. He also started naming things around the tent, and Plexis was proud that one of his first words had been 'horse'.

Nearchus had offered to take Chiron and me on the boat but I didn't want to leave Alexander. I knew the march would be difficult, but it would only be another six weeks and then we'd be in Susa.

We met Craterus's part of the army a few days later. His journey had been long and arduous but he'd lost only about twenty men, all from accidents or sickness. It lifted Alexander's heart to the skies to see all his elephants looking so well.

Roxanne looked well too. She had used the trip to tighten her grip on Lysimachus, the captain of the guards. She hardly even glanced at me, although she knelt at Alexander's feet, playing the role of an obedient Persian queen.

She had mellowed somewhat. I didn't get the sharp looks from her I had in the past, and she sounded almost sincere when she greeted me. She came to my tent soon after I sent for her. I wanted to know what had happened to Paul.

'Ashley! How was your journey?' She was dressed in rich robes and her hair was braided into an intricate crown. For once she was wearing a decent skirt and her breasts were covered. She still wouldn't meet my eyes.

'Fine. Will you have some wine?'

To my surprise, she nodded. 'Thank you.' She took the cup and sipped the wine, moving around the tent, her skirts making a swishing sound as she walked. 'I suppose you want to hear about your son?' It was said with a sigh.

'I want to know why you sent for him, yes.'

'I followed Olympias's order. I didn't dare refuse. If she gave you an order you would have to obey as well, or else be killed.' I said nothing. Roxanne looked at me sharply, but the tight smile she had on her face slipped and faded. 'Can we ever be friends?' she asked me.

I was startled. 'I would very much like to be your friend,' I said. 'But, Roxanne, friendship must work both ways. I can promise you that I will never try to harm you or your children. But will you believe me?'

She flushed. 'If you swore by the goddess your mother, of course I would.'

'Very well. I swear by the goddess my mother I will never try to harm you or your children.'

Roxanne licked her lips nervously. 'I will tell you this then. Olympias has written to me that she and Cassander have made an agreement. They want your son to rule Macedonia. Cassander has no sons, he only has daughters. They want to marry your man-child to Cassander's eldest daughter.'

I gasped. 'But Paul is only ten years old.'

Roxanne flipped her wrist. 'Does it matter? Now I have told you something. Will you tell me something in return?'

'What do you want to know?'

'Will I have more children?' Her voice was carefully neutral, her eyes cast downwards.

'Yes.' I shrugged. It could do no harm to tell her that. 'You will have another son.'

She nodded, but didn't smile. We chatted about the weather, she admired Chiron, who was in his playpen, and then we ran out of things to say. Not surprisingly, I had no idea what I could talk to her about. Poison? Lysimachus? Olympias? Even innocuous subjects like the weather took odd turns with her. She would inevitably tie the conversation into her strange gods, and I never knew what comment to make to a statement such as: 'The rain certainly stimulated Ea. One of my servants died of the bloody flux when she didn't burn a toad on his altar after she stepped in a puddle.' Or, 'One of my nipples is bigger than the other, I think it's because I didn't suckle the monkey's baby long enough. My stupid slave killed it by accident. I've sacrificed to Anahita. Perhaps she'll help me. Otherwise I'll have to kill another one.' *Another what? Slave? Monkey's baby?* I didn't dare ask her to explain anything.

After a few moments of heavy silence, she finished her wine and left the tent. I stood back and watched her leave.

When she was gone, I unclenched my fists. My nails had left little red crescents in my palm.

I didn't let my guard down though, and every gift she sent was instantly tossed in the latrine pit. I was mostly worried about Chiron; he was the biggest threat to Roxanne, and I decided to keep him out of the way of anybody who seemed to have sympathies with her.

Plexis noticed what was going on right away and he became the child's guardian, staying with him whenever I couldn't. Brazza and Axiom helped us in our task, and between the four of us, the little boy was carefully protected.

We were worried about poison, of course, because there were poisons and there were poisons. Some could even be painted on little toys, and there were tiny darts like little bees that stung and killed within hours.


Kalanos, who had been with us since India and who had been with Nearchus on the sea voyage, now rejoined us. He was growing frail, and I worried to see him losing his appetite. He said it was old age.

'Old people don't sleep, and they don't eat,' he said, waving the bowl of lentils away. 'We're turning back into the dust that we came from.' He chuckled; to him death was just another door he would enter.

I told him not to be silly, that he was still a young, handsome man yet, and to eat his soup, please.

He peered at me from under his brows, his black eyes half-mocking, half-sad. 'You will never learn to accept fate.' He sighed. 'For you, life is a battle to be won, not a river to carry you peacefully along. I have tried to tell you this for months. Why will you not listen? When will you learn? We all have to meet our fate.'

I frowned and stared at the steaming bowl of soup, then sighed and ate it myself. 'What if ...' I began slowly. 'What if you knew the future? Would it still be fate? If you could change something, would that mean that fate doesn't exist?'

Kalanos narrowed his eyes. He had the shrewdest stare. He brought to mind the canny gaze of Alexander sometimes, and *he* got that look from Aristotle. 'You cannot cheat fate,' he said. 'What changes you think you have wrought would in fact already be written in the great book of fate. Nothing can be changed. Everything has been ordered since the beginning.'

'But what if I told you I knew what was going to happen?' I cried.

Kalanos smiled gently. 'You think you do, child, but it's like seeing the rapids in the river. You know what rapids are and what they look like, but you've never really been in rapids. You know you're on a river, and perhaps you've seen the whole river in a dream, but it will never be the same until you actually sail upon it. You will see the people, the boats and the fish that the dream cannot show you. You will feel things that knowledge itself cannot make you feel.'

I shook my head stubbornly. 'It's not like that at all,' I said. My eyes were burning. I was in front of an insurmountable wall of belief, and I couldn't get past it. What I wanted to know I couldn't ask outright.

'But it is, and you will see, some day. You must learn to live one day at a time as it comes to you. You must greet each sunrise as a new miracle, and live each instant of each new day as if it will be your last one. Only then can you go forward. Only then can you begin to accept. Once you do, you will find that everything is as easy as breathing. Even dying. From one world to the next, you must learn to go as easily between breathing in and breathing out. Do you remember our breathing lessons?' He leaned forward anxiously. These lessons had been among the first he'd taught us, sitting cross-legged on the rug, taking smooth, deep breaths. Alexander's asthma had improved dramatically since he'd learned to breathe.

'I remember,' I said bleakly. Two tears rolled down my cheeks and fell with audible plops into my soup.

'Lentils not salty enough?' he asked, his eyes twinkling.

'I want to save those I love,' I said. 'It has nothing to do with me. I could let myself go downriver, but I couldn't go and leave those I love behind.'

Kalanos patted my hand. 'You're such a new soul.'

I laughed shakily. I was younger than he by a good three thousand years. My soup got saltier as the tears fell faster.

'I love too,' he said. 'But I have learned to let go. That is the final lesson. You are still too young. No one can ever teach you. It has to be learned alone. When you have learned to let go, then you will be free and you will see that everything that ever held you back from the river's flow hurt you, and everything that let you go forward was beneficial. Love can be both. Will you listen to an old man who has come to the end of his journey?'

'Of course,' I said.

'Let go. Don't try to change what cannot be changed. You will just be swimming against the current and you could drown. Who will look after Chiron when you are gone? I told you once before, gold and silver are not the riches of the earth – the real treasures are children.'

I thought of Paul and my sobs redoubled. Kalanos shook his head pityingly. I was a backward, recalcitrant pupil, but his patience knew no limits. 'Child, child. Dry your tears. Perhaps I am wrong. Real knowledge is believing that you know nothing.'

I looked up at him and tried to smile. 'Well, that's a relief,' I said.

He shook his head some more. 'Ah, I can see that you will do what you believe is right. Didn't you hear me?'

'I did.' I leaned over and kissed his cheek.

'Hey!' He rubbed his cheek, glaring at me. 'You're not supposed to kiss holy men!' His eyes were twinkling though.

'That's my present to you,' I said. 'It's the only thing I have to give to you.'

'That's what you think,' he said. He took my hand, kissed the inside of my palm and folded my fingers over it. 'You keep that. That's the only thing I will give you. You can take it with you downriver, and it will not weigh you down.'

We arrived on the endless plains of Persepolis. We'd camped here, nearly a decade ago. Back then, we'd been chasing Darius, who'd kidnapped our son, Paul. Alexander had met Darius's army on this plain and had triumphed. Barsine had been with us and she'd organized great games on these fields. There had been a stadium, bleachers, and a goatball field. Banquets had been held in the great palace.

Everything had changed. Darius was dead. The stadium had vanished. The palace was in ruins. Now, ten years after Alexander had destroyed the beautiful buildings, dust had swept in and wild asses roamed the echoing rooms. Vines grew along the stairs and over the broken walls. A crushed skull lay by the empty throne, and pale bones had been scattered and gnawed by jackals. Wind whistled through the few marble pillars left standing. Great statues lay in the rubble, their unseeing eyes staring at the sky. White marble sparkled in the sunlight. I clenched my teeth as we approached, and bile rose in my throat. It was a haunting, melancholy place.

Alexander picked his way through the palace. He bent down and dusted off a piece of marble. A young boy's face stared up at him. He jerked backwards, dropping it, then stood and sighed. "Perhaps I should have left it standing," he said. However, I couldn't tell if there was regret in his voice.

We left. I didn't look back.

In Susa, we celebrated another huge wedding. To reward soldiers who had followed him to the ends of the earth and back, Alexander offered money and land to the men who wanted to leave his army. The last wedding at Susa had been an unqualified success, so he repeated it, with ten thousand men and women. All the children who had been born on the voyage were to be provided for until their deaths, and their education was assured by the schools Alexander had founded in each of his cities.

We had arrived in the heart of Persia and the people still reacted with the hysterical fervour of pilgrims seeing their messiah whenever Alexander appeared in public. It was beginning to annoy his Macedonian and Greek generals, who grumbled whenever they could find someone who would listen.

The wedding, however, was quite a festival. Everyone forgot their grievances. For weeks we prepared for the celebration. Cooks baked and barbecued non-stop, festive clothing was made, flowers were woven into crowns and posies, silk was measured and cut, tents were set up, and the scribes were put to work writing marriage certificates. The priests were busy sacrificing, smoke from the altars rose in hundreds of blue spirals into the winter sky, and Plexis married one of Darius's daughters.

The girl had been in Ecbatana with her cousins and her grandmother, but the whole court had come to Susa to welcome Alexander. Darius's mother, Sisygambis, adored Alexander, and was one of the first people to kiss him when he arrived.

Stateira had come from Babylon to be with Alexander. As senior wife, she insisted on staying with him. Alexander was stuck with her now; they were staying in the main quarters of the satrap's palace. I was miserable about that, but I was trapped in the new court protocol, and there was nothing I could do to change it. I was also worn out after the long march, and for some reason I felt depressed and afraid to look towards the future.

I was lodged in a small suite of rooms near the servant's quarters with Brazza and Calanos. Axiom and Usse were with Alexander and Stateira in the Master suite. Roxanne and her court were lodged in one wing of the palace. The women from Darius's court, including his mother Sisygambis and Darius's daughter Drypetis, were in the opposite wing.

Sisygambis had come to see me soon after my arrival. I was pleased to see Sisygambis, or Sis, as everyone called her. She was full of energy and cheerful as a kid goat (another Macedonian saying). She had lost her two sons when they fought against Alexander, but to Sis, war was war, the Persians had been vanquished, and Alexander had won. Furthermore, she'd known Alexander since he was a child and truly loved him. She had sent him mail for the entire time we had been travelling. Letters had come nearly every month following Alexander as he voyaged across the known world. Each letter begged him to take care of himself. They usually included a little prayer, a different amulet, and sometimes a recipe against frostbite, colds, flu, warts, or impotence. We *never* had to bother with that recipe.

Her granddaughter, Drypetis, was a tall, willowy girl with long dark hair. Plexis had been smitten from the moment he saw her, and we teased him unmercifully; the confirmed Athenian bachelor falling for the shy Persian princess. Luckily for Plexis, Drypetis only looked shy. She boldly asked Alexander to marry her to his general, Hephaestion. Their wedding would be celebrated with the ten thousand other soldiers.

Stateira and Alexander were also going to be part of the ceremony. They were planning to be formally married a second time. That's one wedding I was not looking forward to attending, but I was obligated. Roxanne and I would be dressed in identical robes, carry identical posies, and wear identical teeth-gritting smiles. I felt sick just thinking about it.

# Chapter Four

That morning I spent an hour retching miserably into the chamber pot. I drank some mint tea to freshen up, and then I tried to take a nap before the wedding ceremony, but I couldn't sleep. I walked around my apartments picking up objects and putting them down, very much like Alexander when he was nervous. The weather didn't help. Low clouds, pushed by a chilly wind, scudded across the grey sky. The wind whipped away the smoke from the sacrifices, making the priests happy. Supposedly, it was a good sign. Signs were everywhere. The wind was heavy with rain. Two herons had landed in the lake and mated. A man caught a fish with four eyes. A pure white camel with pink eyes was born. I stared out my window and wondered if the signs had always been there, or if I'd just started paying attention to them.

That's when Sis came to pay her respects to me. She was the most maternal woman I'd ever met, and I knew Alexander loved her and thought of her as the mother he'd always wanted. She bustled into my room and held her arms out to me. Her face was wreathed in smiles. She was only slightly afraid of me. She tried not to show it. I hugged her.

I introduced Chiron to her, and she thought he was beautiful. We talked about the four-eyed fish and the forthcoming wedding. She had known Plexis for ages, so she was pleased that Drypetis was marrying him. Then she confided that she hoped that Stateira would bear Alexander many children, because she longed to be a great-grandmother again. She knew I was Alexander's wife. She wasn't being cruel to me. She'd lived her entire life in a harem and shared her husband, the king, with many other wives. She considered them part of her family, and their children were her children. She had never suffered from jealousy and would never understand mine, so I swallowed my pain, smiled, and said I hoped Stateira would bear many children.

Sis wanted to hold a baby in her arms. Chiron loved to cuddle and was feeling sleepy near his nap time, so he was perfectly happy to sit in Sis's lap and doze. She ran her hand through his fair curls, ruffling them.

'Such a lovely boy,' she sighed.

'I'm sorry about Stateira's son,' I said. 'I hope she has recovered from the sorrow of losing the babe.'

'Oh, it took her a while. It was hard; knowing Iskander was so far away and perhaps never even coming back. But she's been patient and ruling Babylon helped keep her from brooding too much. The city is doing very well; she has a real flair for government.' Sis spoke proudly.

'And I heard about Dora, I'm terribly sorry. She was so beautiful.' I was speaking of Darius's wife, a woman reputed to be the most beautiful woman in the world. She had died not long after her husband. Sis had written to tell us, and Alexander had sent money for a huge funeral.

'She *was* lovely, wasn't she? I miss her terribly. She

was as kind as she was beautiful. I would have liked her to have a child, but the gods never willed it. You'll see the rest of the family soon. They are anxious to meet you.'

Sometimes keeping royal families straight was a real exploit. Drypetis, I remembered, had been Darius's youngest daughter. Her mother had been his fifth wife and had died when Drypetis was a baby. Stateira was his eldest daughter by his first wife, who had also died in childbirth.

'Do we go to Ecbatana after the wedding then?' I asked.

'Yes, we want to welcome Iskander to his cities. He'll have to travel all over his kingdom now, showing himself. It's lucky we have such a handsome king. Mind you, we always did have handsome kings. Darius was a handsome man, and so very tall.' She hesitated, frowning. 'Iskander can stand on a wooden box,' she decided.

'He's fine the way he is,' I smiled.

'He is, isn't he?' She sounded pleased. 'Such charisma. Darius was a handsome man, as was his father, but they didn't have half the personality Iskander does. He's such a fiery boy. It's too bad his Greek and Macedonian generals don't seem to worship him as much as the Persians do.' Her eyes grew misty and she patted my hand again. Chiron was now sound asleep in her lap, his thumb in his mouth, his bare feet crossed at the ankles.

The breeze came in the open window and stirred our hair. The air was heavy with rain and I heard the faint sound of thunder in the distance. Clouds were gathering on the horizon. I thought it was apt.

I went to the wedding ceremony with Sisygambis that

night. I'd left Chiron in Axiom's care. Kalanos came to see the great wedding. He had a place of honour in the stands, near Nearchus and the generals. Sisygambis stood between Roxanne and I. I'd managed to ditch my bouquet but chafed in my scratchy bridesmaid dress. Roxanne's eyes fairly smouldered. She had seemed content while apart from Alexander, but now that she was in the same palace, she was plotting on ways to get him back. Her face was pale and her eyes glittered strangely. I thought she looked insane.

Plexis was nervous. His smile wavered and he was alternately blushing and pale. Athenian to the very core, he still felt as if marriage was a yoke around the neck, and Alexander had to talk to him for days before he finally capitulated.

Drypetis looked down demurely at her feet, but her smile was like a cat's that had just found the milk pot. I found my own smile watching them. At least for a few moments. Then my history lessons came crashing down. I suddenly remembered when Plexis was going to die. Not the exact date, but I knew that he had married, moved to Ecbatana, and soon after, he'd died.

I didn't know how, why, or when. But I knew that if I didn't tell Alexander, he would hate me, and if I did tell him, he would despise me. The whole dilemma made me physically ill. Perhaps hearing the name *Hephaestion* pronounced so often jogged my memory. I'd thought of him as Plexis – never as Hephaestion. In the history books, it was Hephaestion who'd died, not Plexis, and it hadn't struck me until the wedding.

I fainted and keeled over in the crowd. Sis was beside me as my eyelids fluttered open. I had been quickly carried to my own quarters, and she had accompanied me. Her face, as she leaned over me, was kind.

'How long have you been ill?' she asked.

'Since this morning,' I groaned. 'Is it something I ate do you think?'

'I don't think so.' She smiled. 'I think Chiron will have a new sibling before next summer. She lifted my tunic and examined my tummy. It was hollow; months of marching hadn't put any weight on me. She shook her head. 'This will never do. You're going to lose the babe if you don't gain weight. You're coming with me to Ecbatana as soon as I leave. Iskander will meet you there.' Her voice brooked no argument.

I sighed. If I were pregnant, I would have to take care of myself. How could I save Plexis as well? If I did anything stupid, the Time Council, that group of historians and scientists who decided when the time-line was in danger, would erase me. So far, I'd been careful. However, time was running out, the grains of sand in the hourglass were falling faster and faster and I felt caught up in a panicked rush.

'I don't want to disturb Iskander on his wedding night,' I told Sis, 'but I must see him tomorrow. Please, send him to me as soon as possible.'

I was stuck in my rooms in the gynaeceum. Actually, for the first few days I hadn't minded staying here. I'd felt more protected and I'd needed the solace of quiet for a while. But now I felt like a prisoner.

Alexander came to see me that evening. He left Stateira and his guests to revel without him and came to my room in the dark. Axiom let him in. There was no surprise on Axiom's face; he had known Alexander would come. He had sent word that I had fainted during the wedding ceremony. I was stunned though. I hadn't expected to see him. I hadn't seen him in three days. When he touched me, I started to weep. I knew why. Now that I knew I was pregnant the signs were obvious. Easy tears, fatigue, illness in the morning, and nervousness.

We lay on the bed and he kissed me. At first I couldn't talk, and then I didn't want to, as our movements quickened and grew more urgent, searching for the release we both knew the other had the power to give. Much later, when I felt the pulse in his neck slow, I was ready to speak, but I still didn't know what to say.

'I'm going to have a baby.' I decided to start with the good news first.

He sat up in the bed. There was enough moonlight coming through the window to show me his face. His eyes were shining. He smiled, and his teeth seemed to glow in the darkness. 'That's wonderful,' he whispered. 'Was that why you fainted during the wedding? I was so afraid that it was because you were upset I'd married Stateira again. However, it made her happy, and I remembered you said that she would die soon after I do. I feel so helpless,' he went on, his voice tightening. 'I wish I could do something. She's a nice enough girl and she would love to stay in Babylon and rule the city. She's quite good at politics actually. Then I thought maybe it was because

Plexis was marrying Drypetis, but no, that's not it.' He went on in a rush. 'You were so happy when he told you he was getting married, and you couldn't have teased him so much if you were truly hurting. Besides, you know how much he loves you and Chiron. I think I was more jealous than you were. When Drypetis asked me if she could marry him, it gave me a shock. I never knew how much I really loved him until ...' He broke off and grimaced. 'I'm sorry. I should let you speak.' His voice was breathless, his colour hectic. I wondered if he were drunk. But there was no wine on his breath, he was simply all nerves.

'I don't know how to tell you this,' I said slowly.

'Is it harder than telling me about my own death?' he asked, a note of teasing in his voice.

'Yes,' I was sad.

He caught my mood and sobered immediately. 'Is it Chiron?' he asked quickly. 'Is he ill?'

'No.' I threw my head back and groaned. 'Oh, no, I can't! I can't do this!' I started to sob.

He grew frightened. 'Is it you?' he asked. 'Are you dying?'

'No. No, I'm fine.' I wiped my eyes. 'It's just something I remembered during the wedding ceremony.'

'During the ceremony, when you were watching me and Stateira? Or Plexis ...' His voice trailed off as he watched my face carefully. I had flinched. 'Is it Plexis?' he breathed.

I put my face in my hands.

'Plexis. Will he die then? Is that it?' It was a whisper. Pain tightened his throat.

'I'm sorry. It was the name. Plexis didn't mean anything to me. I'd never read anything about him. I realized during the ceremony that ... that Hephaestion died.' I choked. My voice broke and it was a minute before I could breathe again. 'I've been living from day to day. For me, it's not history anymore. I was concentrating all my energy on saving you.'

'Can Plexis be saved?'

'How?' I raised my head and stared at him, my face wet. 'Will he accept to leave everything behind? His new wife? His cavalry? Will he accept that I know the future and that he must pretend to die, leave everything behind and disappear from his world? Will he be happy to travel with us, or alone? I'm not even sure I can honestly ask *you* to do all that.'

Alexander's eyes were vacant. He swallowed hard, his Adam's apple bobbing. Suddenly he leaned over the side of the bed and threw up. He was ill, shaking, and a cold sweat covered his body. I called Axiom, and we cleaned up the mess while Brazza took care of Alexander, sponging him off and putting him in the bed under warm covers. Then Axiom gave him some hot tea.

'I'm so sorry,' I said, stroking his hair, pushing the damp curls off his temples and holding him tightly while he trembled.

'I didn't realize what you had to live with,' he said. I wanted to say something but the tone of his voice stopped me. I waited a minute, while he gathered his thoughts, and then he went on. 'I will speak to Hephaestion. I will tell him what I think I can. I will let him decide what he wants

60

to do. Now, tell me, please, when does it happen? How? And mostly, Ashley, why did you tell me?'

'If I didn't tell you, and he had died suddenly, would you have forgiven me?' I asked.

'No, I could not have forgiven you.' His voice was heavy.

I drew in my breath sharply. 'See? You would have wondered all the rest of your life if I could have saved him. But I have no idea why he died, or when. It happens in Ecbatana, I remember that much. Perhaps in two, or three months.'

'So soon?' He shuddered.

'I think so. Listen, Alex, all my life I would have regretted not trying to save him. Because as much as I love you, I love Plexis. You must believe me.'

'It wasn't just a phase then.' He spoke almost lightly, and my tears fell again.

'I was foolish. Love is never a phase,' I said. 'He's the father of my child. I would do anything to save him. But we must also consider the chance that he dies in an unavoidable accident or illness.'

'Well, the same goes for me,' said Alexander, and now his breathing had returned to normal, almost.

We sat for an hour in moody silence. Alexander put his arm around me and pulled me to him. I was glad to lean against his broad chest. My mind was in confusion. I had no wish to put my own life or my children's lives in jeopardy. I was frightened for Alexander, for Plexis, and for my children, and everything was spiralling out of control.

Roxanne sent another present for Chiron, and I'd just managed to intercept it from the messenger before my little boy had come into the room. I shut the door in the messenger's face so he wouldn't see me hiding the toy behind my back. Then I gave it to Brazza washed my hands, and slumped to the floor, shaking. The toy had been a little wooden snake, fully articulated and painted in gay colours. When Brazza had tossed it in the brazier, a large spider had scrambled out of it. I didn't want to tell Alexander, he had enough to worry about. However, Brazza and I had redoubled our watch.

Alexander had his own problems. The schism in the army was becoming increasingly apparent as the Greeks muttered angrily that Alexander was pretending to be a god. Even I had started to hear things.

'You must be careful,' I said to Alexander. 'Your generals have started to grumble and the new scribes are angry because they cannot write about me.'

Alexander was surrounded by journalists now. His newest secretary, Eumenes, was a nice enough man, but terribly meticulous. He insisted on filling in each moment of Alexander's daily life. He was Greek, and although not a sex and scandalmonger like Onesicrite, he was nonetheless concerned with Alexander's private life. 'What should I do? When I'm with Stateira or Roxanne, Eumenes can write all he wants, but I don't know what to tell him about you.'

'Tell him my name is Nobody, and if he wants to fill in the blanks, he can always say you were eating, drinking, or sleeping with nobody.'

Alexander raised his eyebrows. 'People will think I spend all night drinking, and all day sleeping or eating by myself,' he said with a wry grin.

I shrugged helplessly. 'I think that's what they wrote about you anyway.'

'Oh.' He didn't sound happy.

'I'm afraid you'll hate me,' I said.

'Why?'

'Because if I do manage to save you, and you leave, you will always think you've run away. After a while you will begin to believe that I lied. That you weren't actually going to die. That perhaps you would have recovered and all I've ever said has been a lie.' I was whispering now because the pain in my throat wouldn't let me talk.

'No.' He wrapped both arms around me now. 'You said you knew me. So think. Think before you speak in that manner. Have you ever known me to put blame on someone else beside myself for what happens? Have I ever ducked away from my responsibility? I have always faced my fate head-on. I will continue to do so. I know you believe that you can change the course of destiny. I have let you believe I will rise from my deathbed, and that I will leave my empire and my fate. I have betrayed you in a way, so perhaps I had best tell you now. I do not intend to cheat fate. If your hand knocks the cup of poison from mine I will pick it up and drain the cup. I will not touch your potions to heal me. I'm sorry, Ashley. That is my decision. If, despite all these precautions, you do save me, then I will bow to fate because it would have been fate, not you, that saved me. I will leave my crown on the empty throne, and I will go with you.'

'What about Plexis?' I whispered.

'I can't decide for him.'

'Please let me save you,' I begged. 'My life will be worth nothing when you're gone.'

'You will be protected by my men. I will give orders to the ones I trust the most.'

'I want to save you.'

'Don't do anything against my will.' His voice was kind, his eyes full of tears.

'I won't. However, if you die, Iskander, I will throw myself on your funeral pyre and I will die too. I won't live without you. You've made your decision and I have made mine.'

'Oh, my sweet little dream-weaver. Do you really think I'm going to believe you?' His voice broke but there was laughter in it. Laughter, and a terrible tenderness. 'You will never leave your children – our children – to fend for themselves. You must think of Paul. Did I ever tell you how proud I am of him? The first time I saw him my heart leapt for gladness at his beauty and his grace. He is the child of the moon, with his huge, dreamy eyes. There is gentleness in him that the world will never erase. It will be his strength. He reminds me of Kalanos, despite his youth. He will certainly grow up to be a sage, and people will follow him, as they follow me. Only he will lead an army of wisdom, not one of death, like mine.' He tipped his head back, baring his long throat.

'Have you heard from Babylon?' I asked.

'He has not arrived yet. When he does, we will hear from Nearchus.'

'What are you thinking about now?' I asked. His eyes were staring past me, as if he didn't even see me.

'I would dream that I live for ever, and that Paul, Chiron, and the babe in your belly all grow up within my palace.'

'I am your dream-weaver, Iskander,' I said. 'I can make that happen.'

Alexander said nothing to this. Then he spoke. 'You called me "Iskander". Did you hear yourself? That, to me, has always been the name I took with me to war. In times of peace, I wish to be "Alexander". And to you, "Alex".'

'I'll remember that.' I looked past his profile out of the window. A bird had started to sing, making me think dawn was near. 'I'm sorry for all you know about your own future. I wanted you to be the happiest man in the world.'

There was more silence as he thought about that. Then he sighed deeply. 'I must go before the sun rises. I have a busy day ahead of me. Go to Ecbatana with Sis. I will join you in one month. First I must reorganize my army and I fear it will be a long, arduous job. My Greek and Macedonian men are simmering with discontent. They do not wish to adopt Persian customs. The Persians are more flexible in some ways; they eagerly embrace Greek art and literature, and are interested in the philosophy and science. But they are religiously backward and insist on deifying their king. Otherwise they are terrified that the spring will not come to the world nor the sun shine.'

'What will you do?' I asked.

'I have to wait until next summer to prove that the seasons will come regardless if I am a god or not.'

I started to shudder and I thought I would be ill. Next spring he would die. The summer would come without him. I buried my face in his shoulder and keened. My cries were as thin as a wire. I couldn't stop. Nothing he said to me would comfort me. Finally he just stopped talking and rocked me. His tears fell on my back. He was just as miserable as I was.

# Chapter Five

The morning sun woke me. Alexander was gone but the bed still had his warmth and his fragrance. I closed my eyes again and tried to slow my pounding heart. He would not let me try to save him? *Well, we'll see about that*, I thought bleakly. I would not let him die. If I could save him, I would. That was not going to be his decision.

He came to see me in the gynaeceum whenever he had the time. I didn't try to make him feel guilty about leaving me alone. He had so much to do. I only asked one thing in return. When the ambassadors from other countries came, he was to let me listen in on their conversations. He found that a strange request, but agreed; I didn't tell him whom I was waiting for. He never would have believed me anyway.

We celebrated Alexander's thirty-second birthday in Susa. I was hopelessly late giving him a present. His birthday had been nearly three months ago, but I had forgotten it. Everyone had, except Plexis. He'd given him a pure white horse. Pure white horses are genetic oddities. They are not albinos. Their eyes are brown, or china blue. This one had one blue eye and one brown eye. To everyone it could only be the gods' gift for Alexander's kingship.

I gave Alexander a map of the world that I'd

painstakingly drawn. I'm sure everyone knows what the world looks like, but I was no artist. I must have used fifty pieces of parchment before I was satisfied. I used coloured ink and drew in the route we'd taken on our travels. Alexander was thrilled.

'Is this really where we went?' he asked, pointing to the map. 'I thought that I'd gone much deeper into India,' he added, sounding disappointed. 'And I was sure we went further in the boat. Weren't we more over here?' He was looking at the Seychelles.

I giggled. 'No, we didn't get that far. Look, you went from here, Macedonia, all the way to India. You went north as far as the Russian steppes, and south as far as Egypt.'

'I can't believe it was a year ago that we were in the boat. Sometimes it all seems like a marvellous dream. I still see the reef sometimes in my sleep, with the sharks and the bright coral.' He shook his head.

'I know. Time goes too fast,' I said, my throat tightening. He saw my distress and changed the subject.

'Where do the elephants live? The big ones you told me about.'

'Down here, in Africa.'

'And if we follow the Nile we can see them?'

'I promise.' I leaned over to kiss him. He kissed me back, but his finger was already moving across the ocean.

'What's that?'

I had hesitated for a long time before adding North and South America. 'Those are two continents that won't be known to Europeans for another two thousand years,' I explained. 'I was born there.'

'Amazing.' He shook his head. 'Those lands are so huge! How can they remain hidden so long?'

'Because of the oceans,' I said.

'But look, way up here, there is hardly any distance between the two lands.' He was talking about the narrow passage between Alaska and Russia.

'Yes, but that is the great north country I told you about. Ice and snow all year around, and even the sea freezes over sometimes. The distances are greater than they seem. Perhaps a boat could follow the chain of islands here and cross over, but it would be a fearsome voyage.'

Alexander's eyes glittered. 'Wouldn't I love to try it!'

'I thought you hated boats,' I teased.

'Not when they're going somewhere interesting,' he said, shaking his head. 'I have to show this to Nearchus. We must try to get to these lands. Who lives there?'

'The ancients, well, ancient from my time, called them Indians.' When he looked confused, I explained all about the early explorers and their blighted attempts to reach India. 'Everyone wanted to do what you did practically without thinking,' I said. 'You did something absolutely extraordinary.'

He preened, then turned back to the map. 'I don't know if I want to go to Africa and see the elephants, or up here and over here. And what's *this* big place?'

I told him about China, the emperors and the fireworks, and his eyes grew dreamy. Then I told him about Australia, the Great Barrier Reef, and he wondered aloud about a coral reef that was as long as the distance he'd gone between Persepolis and Susa. 'Amazing, amazing,' he kept saying .

'Thank you,' he said, after he'd carefully rolled up the map and tied a silken ribbon around it. 'You have given me the world for my birthday present.'

'I would give it to you for the rest of your life,' I said.

'You don't give up, do you?' he said, laughing gently.

'No. Kalanos said the same thing and my answer is always the same. No. I won't give up. Who are you meeting tomorrow?'

'An ambassador from Iberia.'

'I'm impressed. People are coming from all over the world to meet you.'

We unrolled the map and I showed him where Spain was. Then he wanted me to show him Rome and the North Pole.

'Where is the most dangerous place on earth?' he asked me.

'Right now, or in my time?'

'Now, first.'

I pointed to the heart of Africa. 'Here is a volcanic valley with poisonous gases and dangerous animals. Cannibals live there.'

'What's a cannibal?'

'A person who eats other people,' I said.

He made a horrified face. 'You mean, they kill each other and eat them? It's barbaric!'

'Well, along the lines of human sacrifice and all that stuff, yes, it is pretty awful.'

'And in your time? Where's the most dangerous place?'

My finger hovered over south-eastern Asia. 'Around here. The ground is so saturated with explosive mines that you can't walk five metres without blowing your legs off. Nobody lives there anymore. It's a huge no man's land.'

'Explain.' His voice was curt.

I told him all about the small mines that the countries had scattered all over the earth in the twentieth and twenty-first century. His eyes were incredulous.

'But that's so cowardly!' he cried.

'In my day, war is for cowards,' I told him sadly. 'We could settle everything with reason if we really wanted, but nobody tries.'

'If you could return to your own time, would you go back?'

'Only if I could bring you and my children,' I said.

'*Could* you bring me back with you?'

'I don't think so; the tractor beam is set for a certain weight and mass. It might not work properly for anyone else.'

'Oh. I thought perhaps ...' His voice trailed off.

'What?'

'Nothing. Besides, I would not want to go to see the future. It sounds like such a cold, dreadful place. When you speak of it, you have nothing good to say. All the machines ever invented can't make up for a kingdom covered with bombs, water full of poison, or unbreathable air. You have ruined the future for me.' His voice was brittle, like glass about to shatter.

I turned my face from him, hiding my expression. The future was ruined for me as well. I would hate to return to

71

the dying world I had left. It would be my last choice.

Alexander told me he would talk to Plexis, but I didn't see him for nearly a week and then it was time to leave. I was terribly bored. Life for a Persian princess was gentle and tedious. Slaves served me, dressed me, and sang to me. However, I couldn't show my face outside, and nobody could see me but the other women in the family and my own husband. We had to tell everyone that Axiom was a eunuch. Otherwise, he would have been executed for daring to set eyes upon me. He was very careful how he shaved.

I was happy to leave Susa. I thought that I'd have more freedom in Ecbatana.

Plexis and Drypetis left as well. He had been appointed satrap of Ecbatana and he would rule there with Drypetis. Most people thought the solution ideal. Ecbatana was in the north near the tribes of Artabazus and Pharnabazus, who raised the horses for the army. In addition, everyone knew that Plexis was a consummate horseman. Some muttered angrily that Plexis didn't deserve the post, which was an important one, because Ecbatana was the seat of the treasury as well. Plexis couldn't care less about the huge treasure stored in it, but there were men who had dreamed of taking care of that, and to see someone put in charge who was more interested in horses than gold was intolerable for them.

I travelled with the women. I had to ride in a curtained litter. I carried Chiron in my arms and thought of my leave-taking. I had bade goodbye to Alexander in front of a strangely silent crowd. It was the first time I'd seen him in days, and our farewell was public. I had to bow down to him and press my face to his feet. He had to pretend he didn't even see me. I wore a veil that covered my face. I abhorred it. I felt as if I was suffocating. Alexander's eyes were bleak. I did not cry, I hated showing any weakness.

With me were Axiom, Brazza, and Chiron. Usse stayed with Alexander, Kalanos as well. We would meet in Ecbatana in a month. Stateira stood on the right of Alexander; Roxanne was on his left. I ground my teeth in frustration. I was leaving Alexander and we hadn't had another chance to speak about Plexis. I didn't know what Alexander had said to him, or if he'd even spoken to him at all. I had warned Usse to watch out for Roxanne and for poison. Now all I could do was wait. Alexander would join us in less than a month. Until then, I had to plan. More importantly, I had to try to speak with Plexis.

# Chapter Six

For two weeks, we journeyed. The weather was hot. Sullen clouds darkened the sky, but the storm didn't break. It seemed to gather instead. Sometimes lightning would flicker across the plains. It was strange, green lightning, and the electricity in the air made everyone tense. In the distance, I saw herds of wild asses, but otherwise there was nothing to see but dust devils whirling on the plains, and sometimes I saw great flocks of birds, their cries echoing in the vastness of the skies.

The land we crossed was devoid of interest at first, but lavender hills were visible in the distance. My curtained litter was uncomfortable and I was restless. I had refused Sis's offers of ladies-in-waiting, and now I was starting to regret it. Chiron wasn't the greatest conversationalist. If there were people around, or if we were going through a village, whenever I parted the curtains the guard ordered me to close them. I found myself closed in more often. We were climbing into the mountains, it was cooler and there were more settlements. We were approaching the city, and I hadn't had time to see Plexis. I hadn't the right to see anyone. It would have been impossible to stroll into Plexis's tent. We were in Persia now, not with Alexander's army. Strict protocol had taken over and I was guarded day and night. At night, when we camped, Axiom and Brazza

74

guarded me inside my tent. Outside, when we marched, the Persian guard watched over me. The royal women were cloistered and could not be looked upon by anyone but their husbands, so the royal Persian guards took their job seriously. Under Persian law, any man setting eyes on my face would be blinded, whether Alexander ordered or not. I was expected to stay veiled and hidden. If I were found with a man, I would be put to death immediately. The guard might hesitate a second, but only a second. The man I was found with would be tortured, then put to death.

The royal women had to hide their faces behind veils. The other Persian women were free to wear what they liked and most wore lavish clothes and cosmetics. They could go to the theatre and the horse races, and they could ask for a divorce and own property. The royal women, ironically, had no rights. They had to remain veiled and hidden, could never get a divorce, and couldn't even leave their quarters unless the order was given. The royal wives could only watch as other women went to the market, went swimming in the river, or rode their donkeys to visit with friends and family.

I might never have seen Plexis alone, but Drypetis discovered she was pregnant and asked to stay with her grandmother's cortège. I decided to take advantage of her absence. I put on Axiom's robes and hid my bright hair. The night was dark. I had Axiom lean out and say aloud, 'Excuse me, my lady, I must go and speak to Hephaestion.' Then he pulled his head back in the tent and I rushed out under cover of night. The guards thought I was Axiom and waved me through. I darted into Plexis's tent.

He wasn't sleeping. He was lying on his bed reading. When I came in, he looked up, polite interest on his face. He wasn't expecting any visitors. When I took my hood off, he sat up in surprise. 'Ashley!' he cried, then he frowned. 'Why did you come?'

'I need to speak to you. Before I say anything else, I want to congratulate you. I heard Drypetis is expecting a child. I'm so happy for you, Plexis, she's a lovely woman.'

'I know.' He smirked and lay back on his bed. He had regained most of the weight he'd shed on our hard journey. Two months of feasting and rest had filled the hollows in his cheeks and erased his ribs. Naked, he lay sprawled on his covers. His hair was tousled and his eyes were bright, but I fought the urge to join him. I wandered around his tent, picking up his helmet, turning it over in my hands, then setting it down. I touched a small bronze horse that I'd given him as a wedding present. Drypetis had decorated the tent with her affairs but the little horse had the place of honour. There was an altar with the votives and statues of several deities on it. Drypetis was a normal, religious girl. I didn't think Plexis would ever leave her. And now she was expecting his child. My feelings for Alexander's other wives or lovers were complex. I'd gotten to like Barsine immensely and although I didn't care for Stateira, she only inspired pity in me. As for Roxanne, the only feeling I could dredge up for her was wariness. Strangely enough, I was jealous of Drypetis. My eyes blurred with tears. A crown of flowers was on the table. I kept my back turned to Plexis and fingered the fragrant blossoms.

He moved silently. I never heard him. He grasped my shoulders before I even knew he was behind me.

'Tell me,' he commanded.

His body pressed against mine and I felt the familiar spark of attraction working again. How easy it would be to turn and find myself facing him, his chin level with my forehead. He was not much taller than I. He was built lightly, like a dancer. My bones were shaking. 'I can't.'

'Not until I'm on my deathbed.' It was said lightly, but his grip tightened on my arms. 'When will that be?'

'Soon, Plexis.' It was a whisper. Now my nose was bleeding .

He turned me around and cupped my face in his hands. His hazel eyes were full of pity. 'I never envied you your knowledge,' he said.

'And I never envied you your own gift,' I said. 'You know, don't you, what I'm trying to tell you?'

'Iskander came to me before I left.' He pulled me to him. The blood on my face left scarlet ribbons on his shoulder. He smoothed my hair, leaving a trail of blood in that too. Suddenly my knees gave away. Everything was red, everything was covered with blood. I was crying tears of blood, drowning in a river of it.

It was nothing but a vision, brought on by the stress and the faint. Plexis carried me to his bed and he took soft linen to clean my face.

'What do you want to do?' I asked him.

He leaned down and kissed me. 'I want to make love to you one last time. Will you let me? Please?'

'No.' My voice broke. He looked at me, surprised. 'I

want to know what you understood. I want to hear what Alexander said, and I want to know if you really want it to be the last time. Oh, Plexis, I can't bear it!' I curled up on my side and sobbed.

His breathing was even, light, his eyes sad. His face was pale in the blue light. Somehow, he'd found a lamp like the one we used to have in our tent. He looked like he was underwater in the blue-green light. His mouth, with its deep curls at the corners and the full lips, was serious. His expression, usually so puckish, was grave now.

He laid a hand on my breast. 'He told me that I would die soon but, that you might be able to cheat fate. He said that perhaps you would speak to me. He wasn't sure. He thought maybe you would rather watch and see what happens. He said that if I did live, I would have to give up everything and disappear.' A faint grin made a dimple appear. I stared at it; I'd never noticed it before. 'I didn't know that I could just disappear,' he said, conversationally. 'I thought it would be difficult to become invisible.'

'Don't be facetious,' I murmured.

'That's what Iskander said.' His dimple deepened then vanished. He laid his head on my breast, his hand sliding down to my waist, then dipping between my legs. I gasped involuntarily and my back arched. 'I'm not sure I want to disappear.' His mouth found my nipple. He stroked me, gently, until my breathing was as harsh as his had become. 'I don't want to talk anymore,' he said, and he rolled onto me, claiming me with his body. I closed my eyes. Plexis would always have the ability to make me forget my pains, my hurt, and myself. That was his gift. That, and the ability to see into the shadows that normally only the sibyls could pierce.

My gift was that I could make him lose himself. He hung back, but I could pull him with me over the edge. I bit his shoulder hard enough to make him cry out, and our lovemaking degenerated into a tussle that flung us off the bed and across the rug. The table tipped and the flowers fell over us in a shower of yellow and white petals. The smell of the fragrant blossoms, crushed under our straining bodies, mingled with our soft cries. I felt the wave cresting and I arched up to meet it. Plexis bowed his head into me and we met in the middle. There was a clap of thunder. I wasn't even sure where I was until I opened my eyes. The rain was rushing in the open tent flap, and Drypetis was standing, staring at us, her face a frozen mask of horror.

I looked up at Plexis. His chest and shoulder were smeared with blood from my nose. His face was perfectly blank. I couldn't tell if he was horrified or furious. Or totally destroyed.

There was nothing I could say. It wasn't his fault she'd come back to get her amulet – the one that would protect her from demons. And it wasn't her fault that a woman could be killed if she was unfaithful to her husband, and that kings' wives were taboo. Nobody had the right to touch me. In her eyes, her new husband and I had committed a heinous crime.

She opened her mouth to scream and Plexis acted without thinking. If the guards were called, if they came in and found us, they would kill me first. Then Plexis would be tortured and killed. He had no choice. He leaped at her, grabbed her around the waist, and cupped his hand over her mouth. 'Will you promise not to scream?' he asked.

She nodded, her pupils huge. As soon as he let her go, she backed away from him as if he were a huge, hairy spider.

I reached towards her but she spat at me. 'How could you? You are Iskander's wife!' She clapped her hands over her own mouth. 'You deserve to die!' Her eyes were hard as black stones. I couldn't believe I'd ever thought of them as soft black velvet.

'I won't die if you say nothing,' I said warily.

'I said you *deserve* to die.' She wiped at her face now, as if to scrape off the imprint of Plexis's hands. 'So do you,' she said to her husband. 'How could you? How could you touch Iskander's wife? How could you dare?'

'What will you do?' I asked carefully.

She was breathing in great gulps. Her mouth was twisted with a mixture of fury and fear. Then she hissed, 'Roxanne warned me to watch out for you. She said you had ruined her marriage and she told me you would try to do the same for mine.'

'I didn't ruin anything,' I said desperately. 'Iskander never loved Roxanne but Plexis loves you. Don't throw that away. Please, listen …'

'From what I can see, it is not the first time,' she said.

I stared at her distrustfully. Suddenly she took a deep breath, as if to scream. I don't know if she meant to call the guards but Plexis thought so. He clamped his hands over her mouth again. She struggled and kicked, shaking her head back and forth, her cries muffled. Finally he uttered an oath and cuffed her on the side of the head. Her eyes rolled up and she slumped to the ground. Plexis knelt by her, stroking her cheek. I couldn't tell what he was thinking.

'Is she all right?'

'Yes. She'll wake up with a headache, that's all.' His voice was a whisper.

'Plexis, I'm sorry.' I was breathing hard, as if I'd been running very fast. 'I seem to be able to ruin your life in an instant. And Iskander's too. I ruined his life for him. I wrecked his future. That's what he told me. That I'd made the future a cold, dark place.' I looked up at him. My nose bled slowly, dripping down my chin. 'I'm a curse,' I said.

Plexis gaped at me. Then he crossed the tent and took my arm. 'You're not. I promise. But you mustn't be found here. It's too dangerous. I don't know what came over me; we've been too long with the army. Leave, please, just go. I'll deal with Drypetis.'

I shook my head. 'No. I won't let anything happen to you. Maybe it will be better if I am killed. Then, when you and Iskander die we can all be together again.' My voice was shrill.

'Shh, hush. Listen, I know what you were trying to tell me. I'm not very good with things I don't understand. Like women. Give me a horse any day. However, I have Chiron to think of. And Iskander. Let us wait until he comes and we'll talk, just the three of us. But until then, you will go back to your tent.'

'I told Iskander that I loved you as much as I loved him,' I said.

81

'You did?' He smiled faintly. Then he looked down at Drypetis, lying on the floor, her hair spread out in a black cloud around her face. 'I was infatuated with my wife,' he sighed. 'I thought that I would grow old surrounded by my children and on late winter evenings I would lean back in my bed and remember my love affair with the Goddess, and those thoughts would warm my bones and comfort me.' He took my hand and pressed it to his lips. 'I love you, but I never told you. I'm sorry.'

'I know you loved me,' I said sadly.

'I still do.' He moved into my arms and pressed my cheek to his chest. 'I will listen to you when the time comes, if you wish.' His body trembled against mine and I closed my eyes.

'I want to have you near me always,' I said. 'I'd better go, she's waking up.'

He kissed me before I left and he said, 'I'm sorry I said anything about making love for the last time. I was wrong.' He smiled and there were sudden tears in his amber eyes. 'Did you tell Iskander you loved me as much as you love him?'

'I did, and I meant it.'

He grinned crookedly as I left, pulling the cloak over my head. In the storm nobody saw me, or if they did, they assumed it was Axiom.

# Chapter Seven

The rest of the voyage passed quietly. It lasted only three more days and Drypetis was silent for the whole time. She was suffering from shock. It wasn't her fault, and it wasn't that she minded Plexis making love with another woman. He could take more wives if he wished. Under Persian law, polygamy was allowed, and she had been raised in a harem. Plexis was Greek. He would never have taken another wife. What had shocked Drypetis was the crime he'd committed, a crime punishable by death. When we got to Ecbatana, she went straight to the women's quarters without asking to see Plexis. Sisygambis noticed. She noticed everything. Sis went to see Drypetis, who told her grandmother about Plexis and me.

The nice thing about Ecbatana was the women's palace. Instead of being small suites of rooms, like in Suze, here the women had a huge building for themselves. It held a garden as big as a park, with sparkling fountains, thousands of flowers and colourful, squawking parrots. I'd been in the palace for two days before Sisygambis, or Sis as she liked to be called, paid me a visit.

I was in my bath when Sis found me. I had a huge, sunken marble bathtub full of warm water and rose petals. Chiron was splashing and playing with a wooden boat that Plexis had made for him. In a week, he would be three years old. He had been born in the Hindu-Kusch, had travelled to India, and crossed the desert to Persia. A real explorer. I smiled at him, and pushed the boat back in his direction.

'Hello, Ashley.' It was Sis. She stood uncertainly in the doorway, her hands clasped in front of her. It was so unlike her to appear unsure of herself, that I knew right away what it was about.

'I'll be right with you,' I said. I motioned to one of the slave girls, and she brought me a robe. I gave Chiron to Axiom, and then I braided my hair as Sis and I walked towards the balcony. We could speak privately there.

When we were seated on a low bench with a tray of cool lemonade set in front of us, Sis cleared her throat.

'My dear, I don't want to seem disapproving. However, you must never see Hephaestion again. Drypetis wants to tell Iskander everything, and I managed to persuade her that it was unnecessary. She would lose a husband, and you would lose your life.'

'But Sis,' I said with a smile. 'Alexander doesn't mind.'

She looked at me, her mouth a perfect "O". Then she nodded her head quickly, which meant "No". 'Of course you don't know what you're saying. However, I will try to make this absolutely clear. You are pregnant. You have been unfaithful. By our laws you should die. Nevertheless, I will protect you. Drypetis will say nothing. Not even to Roxanne.'

I gave a strangled gasp. 'If you love Iskander even a little,' I said, 'never, ever let Roxanne know. She will—' I broke off, not sure how much I could say.

Sis patted my hand. 'I do love Iskander. That's why I will try to save your life. And I love Drypetis, so I will save Hephaestion's life. You will stay in your quarters until your baby is born. Then you will be sent to join Iskander wherever he may be. He will give orders when he gets here.'

'Will I see him when he arrives?' I asked, growing panic making a hard lump in my throat.

'If he asks for you. And child, we must get rid of Axiom. Everyone knows he's not really a eunuch. Why didn't you take only Brazza? Furthermore, I meant what I said about staying in your quarters. You may not walk around the palace anymore. You've upset Drypetis so much she's in danger of losing her baby.' Her face was kind, she meant well.

I felt my sanity starting to slip. Alone here until my baby was born? Alexander would be dead by then! If I could never see Plexis again, how could I save him? He would die before I could even try to save him. What about Paul? If Alexander and Plexis died, who would protect him? My panic started a nosebleed, which frightened Sis.

'By Ishtar! Another prophecy!' she shrieked.

It was the best thing that could have happened. I closed my eyes and stood up. In a deep voice I intoned, 'You will leave Axiom here. He protects Iskander's child. Ashley must be allowed to leave her quarters. Demeter's daughter may not be kept like a beast in a cage, no matter how lovely the cage. The goddess has spoken.'

I sat down and then gave a huge start, pretending to

wake up. 'Did I say something?' I asked, blinking and looking around as if confused. I put my hand to me face and stared at the blood. 'Oh! My mother, Demeter, has sent another message! What did she say this time?'

Sis was green. For the people of that time, the gods and goddesses were just a hair's breadth away from reality. They could appear any minute. There were regular sightings, quite like the UFOs in my time. The gods could come to earth and make love to girls. I imagined a few unexpected pregnancies were hastily explained in this fashion. The resulting baby was given the best of care. Priests and priestesses spoke to gods regularly, and the sibyls in their smoky oracles conversed with Apollo. It was an interesting time to live. The people were like five-year-olds believing in Santa Claus. They *really* believed. And when the five-year-old sees Santa sitting in the mall, surrounded by plastic reindeer and fake snow, does the five-year-old doubt? No, he does not. Depending on his mettle he either shrieks with joy or screams in panic, and that's how the people here reacted to the gods.

Sis panicked before the gods. Many down-to-earth people who pride themselves on their common sense lose it when confronted with the supernatural. Axiom stayed with me. I could walk around the women's palace as I pleased.

I asked Axiom to get me three things: a black wig, men's robes, and a pair of scissors.

I cut off my shining hair. It had been growing for ten years and had reached my waist. It was a shimmering, silky waterfall of pure platinum, and far too easy to spot. I braided it and made it into a hairpiece. I didn't want anyone to know I'd cut it off.

I dressed in men's robes, put on the black wig, and used charcoal to make a rough sort of five o'clock shadow on my cheeks. Very dashing. Axiom closed his eyes and prayed to his one god to spare me.

Nobody was watching the window from where I escaped. It wasn't a very important one. The windows in my rooms were watched by guards day and night, but I'd discovered a long-forgotten window behind a thicket of jasmine. The garden had grown up so luxuriously that some parts were hidden from sight, and no one bothered with them. The palace itself was so vast that it was surrounded by a myriad of streets. Some were big, and some, like the one outside this window, were nothing but glorified alleyways. Somehow, Axiom had procured a ladder, and he held it while I clambered down to the street. Then I pushed the ladder behind the vines growing up the wall and waved cheerfully to Axiom.

I straightened my robes and made sure my wig was set firmly on my head. Thankfully, Persian men wore more clothes than the Greeks. The Greeks walked around nude most of the time, or with short capes slung over their shoulders. Very sexy, but impractical for a woman impersonating a man. Here in Persia the robes were voluminous, down to the ankles, and the men wore funny hats. I'm serious. Any hat that looked bizarre was considered 'chic'. Turbans, cone-hats, flat discs, wide brimmed hats, well, you name it. If it looked odd, it was great. I had a blue silk turban. It was like a giant mushroom on my head.

Ecbatana was lovely. The largest buildings were made of pink stone and brick, with charmingly painted murals. Trees shaded the streets. The city was set up with the palaces in the centre. The marketplace formed a large rectangle built on the banks of a small river. Boats carried all sorts of produce to and from the city. It was also an important caravan stop, and the market was a huge, sprawling affair.

I bought a handful of dates and nibbled on them as I wandered around. I loved markets, and this one was one of the best I'd ever seen. Surrounding it were different sized temples, one for each god in the Persian pantheon. Some temples were big, elaborate buildings, and some were small, unimposing huts – depending on the importance of the god it housed. In the huge square, set up in straggly lines, were hundreds of small stands with merchants loudly hawking their wares. Small fountains cooled parched throats. Brightly coloured awnings gave ample shade, and four wide avenues led from the market to the four sides of the walled city.

I strolled along the brick walkway following the river. Stairs led to the water where boats were tied to iron rings, and where traders sat on their boats and sold everything from apples to zebra skins. Apples were common, while zebra skins were very rare and exceedingly expensive.

The tall buildings along the waterfront were beautiful. They were painted deep rose with blue and yellow trim. Potted palms grew on balconies, the rooftops were silver-plated, and flowers were everywhere. The city was prosperous and peaceful. Its noises were comforting; there were the loud cries of the merchants advertising their wares, the high voices of women fetching water in earthenware jugs, the shrieks and laughter of children, dogs barking, and the bright chatter of people bargaining for goods.

It was October. The air had a brassy feel to it; an autumn smell of ripe apples and grain. The heat had dried the plains, and dust made the sunsets a riot of reds and oranges. Dust pervaded the air and it glittered faintly gold.

The river water was deep and amber-coloured. In the evening, fishermen cast their lines off the banks and bridges and waited for the fish to bite. Beggars sat on the steps of the temples. On one of the fountain walls a youth did handsprings. Minstrels sang for coins. A man sliced oranges and squeezed juice for drinks. Earthenware cups lined his stand and I bought a cup of juice, drank it, and gave the cup back. He rinsed it in the fountain and filled it with bright juice again. On another table were slices of frosty pink watermelons.

As the blue evening gathered coolness around the city, I found a man reading the news. He was standing near the steps of the courthouse on a large block of stone. At his feet was a small hat full of coins. He held a rolled-up parchment in his hands. He was waiting for a client.

'Good evening,' I said, making my voice gruff. 'What news have you?'

He unrolled the parchment and harrumphed, giving a quick glance at the hat near his feet in case I didn't understand. I tossed a silver coin in with the rest and he smiled broadly. 'For that you get all the news and the latest gossip from the palace,' He said. 'Let's see, first of all, the prices. Oil and …'

'No, skip the prices,' I said, 'I'm not buying or trading. Get to the news.'

'Fine, no problem. Let's see. Iskander, our mighty king, has been spotted three days' march from the city. He will arrive with his court and most of his famous generals. If you want autographs, go to the palace; in four days there will be an open-air meeting. Anyone can attend. The army has stayed behind in Susa. The biggest news happened in Opis not a week ago. Iskander wanted to retire his oldest Macedonian generals and replace them with Persians. The Macedonians and the Greeks rebelled. A great scuffle occurred and several men were killed. Iskander made a very long speech after that, the gist of it being this … hold on …'

He took another parchment out of his leather pouch and unrolled it. Clearing his throat dramatically, he read, ' *"All the resources of Cyrene and Egypt are yours. Syria, Palestine and Mesopotamia are your kingdoms now. Yours are Susa, Babylon, Bactria, the riches of Lydia, the treasures of Persia, the wealth of India, the great ocean. You are satraps, generals, commanders; and of all this, what remains for me? For all my pain and struggles, what is mine except for the purple robe and crown I am wearing? I possess nothing for myself, and nobody can point to any treasures belonging to me except what belongs to you as well, and which I guard for you. It's not for my personal use I guard them, seeing I eat the same* food you do, and even quite a bit less than you. I even wake earlier than you, so that you may rest in the mornings.

"So, tell me! Who among you has worked harder than I do? Who has endured more pain and suffering? Who has fought harder for me than I fought for them? So? Will those with scars take off their robes and show me, and I will show mine! There is no part of my body, in front or back, which bears not the marks of battle! I have been wounded by sword, by lance, by arrows, by catapults, and hand-to-hand fighting! And all that was for your glory! I have made you lords of the mountains and plains, of the rivers, seas and forests. My weddings were celebrated with yours, and many of my children and yours are related.

"I told you I wished to send those of you back who were no longer fit for active service. To send you back with enough honours and gold to make you the envy of your entire village. Now you tell me you all wish to go? So be it. Go, all of you! But when you reach your villages tell them this; tell them that your king, the same Alexander who vanquished the Persians, the Medes, the Bactrians, the Scythians, who subdued the Uxians, the Arachosians, the Zarangians, who captured the Parthians, the Hyrcanians to the Caspian sea, who crossed the Caucus mountains, the rivers Oxus, Tanais and Indus; where only Dionysus went before, and who would have crossed the Hyphasis had you all not refused out of fear. The same Alexander who went to the outer sea from the two mouths of the Indus, who crossed the Gedrosian desert where none had crossed before, whose navy sailed the coast of the Persian sea, and *who brought you all back to Susa. This Alexander, whom you wish to abandon and whom you will leave to the protection of the barbarians he conquered. Be sure, when you announce this, men will celebrate your valour and the gods your piety. Go now! Leave me!".'*

'He said all that?' I was impressed. It sounded like something Alexander would say when he'd lost his patience and his temper. I wondered who had started the rebellion and who had been killed. 'What happened next? Did his generals desert him?' I asked.

He looked at me pityingly. 'Would they do that? No, of course not. There was a huge feast the next evening and all the generals cried and begged forgiveness. They just wanted him to see that they were jealous of the Persians, that's all.' He shrugged. 'But we're in Persia, after all, and Iskander is trying to please everyone, as usual.'

'Very astute,' I said, peering closely at the man. 'What else is new?'

'Let's see.' He rolled up the speech and took his first parchment. 'There will be a play about Epaminondas and his Democratic Party tonight at the theatre, and afterwards a debate about how the Greeks and Persians differ and how we can learn to live together. It will be animated by the B.R.B.G.P. society, better known as *Better Relations between Greeks and Persians*. There is a sale on parrots over by the temple, and anyone finding a white dog who answers to the name of Rex is asked to bring him to the Greek consul, where his master waits. A reward of ten obols is offered. And it says here that Plato died.'

I frowned. 'That was over twenty years ago!'

'News travels fast nowadays,' said the man proudly.

'What's the gossip in the palace?' I was curious.

'Very interesting news. Supposedly Iskander's wife, Demeter's daughter Persephone, is there, though nobody has seen her. She will be prayed to in Ishtar's temple; the priestess is thinking about changing it to Demeter's temple. A vote will be held in four days' time. Drypetis is expecting her first child. She is doing poorly and has been confined to her bed.'

I was startled; I hadn't seen her around, but I hadn't known she was ill. 'Poor girl!' I said.

The man nodded sympathetically and continued. 'The men in the palace are organizing a huge celebration for Iskander's arrival, including polo games and an elephant parade. Hephaestion is looking for volunteers for the polo games, anyone with experience and good horses can contact him at the palace.'

I remembered that Plexis had left his precious cavalry in Susa. *He must miss them terribly*, I thought. Then I sighed. He was as alone as I was. He was the new ruler of Ecbatana. He had people coming to see him constantly. However, none were his friends. When you are on top, everyone below looks up avidly waiting for you to topple so that they can tear you to pieces.

The newscaster was looking at me closely. 'Nice eyes you have there,' he said. 'Unusual colour. Like the early morning sky on a freezing winter's day.' He shivered. 'Nice, but terribly chilly.'

'Are you a poet?' I asked. I wasn't looking at him though. I was staring at the other side of the river, at the field where huge stands were being set up for the games. The city was getting ready to receive her king. Iskander was marching to Ecbatana. So many things were coming to a head. I shook my head suddenly, startled by tears that trickled down my cheeks.

'Your beard is washing away,' said the man. 'Here, take my hankie.'

'Thank you.' I wiped my eyes and dabbed at my face. 'Is it better now?'

'No, there's a streak here.' He took the hankie and brushed my cheek. 'There, now it's fixed. You should be careful, try not to get upset.'

'It's normal, I'm pregnant,' I told him, grinning wryly.

'Really? Is it a miracle or are you perhaps not the man I thought you were?' He chuckled at his own joke.

'Tell me something, how do you get your palace gossip?' I was curious.

'I have my sources,' he said, puffing his chest out. 'Seriously, do you think I'd tell you?'

'Why not?'

'True, why not? I'll tell you then. It's the chief eunuch's slave-boy. He tells me everything when he comes shopping for incense every morning.'

'Why did you tell me?' I asked. 'Aren't you afraid I'll tell someone?'

'Who? You're obviously not from around here. Your accent is atrocious by the way. You sound like a ...'

'I know what I sound like,' I held up my hand. 'A lousy actor playing a Mesopotamian whore. So what else is new?'

He grinned. 'I like you Mr. Missus whatever you want to be. Therefore, I'll tell you a secret. There's a plot to do away with the new satrap, Hephaestion. He's not very popular with the Persians. Too Greek by far. The eunuch, Bagoas, is plotting against him.'

'Bagoas? But why?' I gasped. Bagoas was rumoured to be the most beautiful man in Persia. I'd never seen him, but Alexander had told me about him. This was terrible news. I glanced up at the newsman who was staring at me with narrowed eyes.

He leaned closer and said in a low voice, 'I heard it's because he's jealous. Supposedly, he tried to seduce Iskander years ago, when he was here last time, and told Iskander he wanted to rule Ecbatana. He was waiting for that post, but Iskander put Hephaestion in charge. Bagoas swore he'd get even for that slight. Amazing what I know, isn't it?' He grinned.

'How does he mean to kill him?' I asked. 'Poison?'

Now he whispered into my ear. 'He means to kill him during the games. I don't know how. I'll ask the slave-boy tomorrow, so meet me here. Same place, same time. I'll tell you everything I can find out.'

'Thank you,' I said, putting another coin in his hat. He looked at me, amazed. I'd put a gold coin in it.

I walked back in a daze. The sun had set, and the whole city was lit by street lamps made of pink blown-glass. The city was enveloped in a rosy glow. There was still a thin red line to the west. It shimmered like a fire on the very edge of the world. The buildings gave off the day's heat. I put my hand on a brick wall. It felt almost alive. The flowers released their scent and the air was heavy with jasmine and heady gardenia. Their waxy white blooms peeped out of deep green foliage. I pushed aside a swath of jasmine vine and uncovered the ladder I'd left under the window. A glance showed me the alley was empty, and I scrambled up to the window. I made sure the ladder was well hidden again before I took off my disguise and washed my face in the basin of water I'd left behind the palm tree. Then I folded my clothes and slipped into my own apartments. I took great care now. I didn't trust anyone.

*Bagoas*. I frowned. I had never seen him. He was reputed to be so handsome that woman swooned and men fought each other for the right to court him. He held a great deal of power, and I guessed that the last satrap must have been his pawn. Poor Plexis. He was more at home on a horse than in a palace. What had possessed Alexander to give his friend this post?

I found Axiom and told him everything I'd found out. Chiron was in bed, sleeping. I'd been gone for a long time. Axiom, the only one who knew what I was up to, had been worried. He was relieved when he saw me sneaking in the room. We hadn't even told Millis, the eunuch Sis had given me when I arrived in Ecbatana. I didn't trust anyone, and I was afraid he was her spy. Millis was Darius's son by a slave woman, and therefore a slave, although his father had been the most powerful man in Persia. Being born male, in a harem, he was castrated when he was seven. His tongue was cut out, to keep him from speaking, and he was trained in the art of massage and lovemaking.

In the gynaeceum, the women were often bored but rarely frustrated. Eunuchs guarded them, and slept with them. Sis had given me Millis, her own grandson. She would never think of him as her grandson, however. He was a slave, and that was all he'd ever be for her. I could never understand. I thought Millis was the most handsome person I'd ever seen, but when he tried to make love to me I told him, in no uncertain terms, that I only wanted a back rub. He was a wonderful masseur. He was mute, but not deaf. He adored me, and followed me around constantly. I liked him well enough. He was wonderful with Chiron too, but I wished he would stop insisting on sleeping at the foot of my bed. I hated it. Millis, however, seemed to think it was the highest honour I could give him – except maybe letting him sleep with me, and I wasn't about to do that – so every night he unrolled his pallet out on the floor and curled up to sleep. Actually, I wouldn't have minded too much if he did sleep. But he didn't. He lay there staring at me.

'Millis! Go to sleep!' I would hiss, and he'd close his golden eyes for a second. Then he would open them again and watch me, as if he were afraid I'd disappear during the night. It had occurred to me that Sis had asked him to make sure I didn't leave the gynaeceum.

The next day I changed my disguise and went to town dressed as a youth. It was easier to do with my smooth cheeks. I still wore a wig but I cut it short, and instead of a funny hat, which marked me a married man, I wore a simple linen bandanna around my head. I had a knife tucked in my belt which meant I was a free man. I wouldn't have minded going as a slave, but slaves were expected to look busy, not idle around, and I wanted to wander. I hadn't finished exploring the city, and I had to get the latest news. I had sent Millis on an errand, so I wasn't worried about him.

When the afternoon shadows grew long I went to the courthouse and found my newscaster. He was sitting on a woven grass mat, his back to the block of stone, gnawing on a lamb chop. 'Well, you certainly have changed,' he told me. 'You seem to get younger each time I see you.'

I smiled uncertainly. 'Do you have any news for me?'

'I do, actually.' He tossed the bone to a passing dog. 'Is that you, Rex?' But the dog only grabbed the bone and slunk away.

'That dog wasn't white,' I reminded him.

'That's true, but if he's anything like you maybe he decided to change his coat.' He stretched his arms and cracked his knuckles. 'Bagoas means business. He's going to do something during the polo match but I know not what. The slave-boy was unwilling to give me any details. It seems Bagoas is gifted in poisons and many of his servants have died young.' The man paused and glanced at his hands. 'Perhaps it is not for me to say, but if I were you I would beware Bagoas. He has long arms and some say he can reach into the very heart of the gynaeceum.' He said this blandly, but his eyes were sharp.

I grimaced. 'Is it so obvious?' I asked.

'No, my lady, but you shouldn't leave the protection of the walls of your apartments. There are spies everywhere. Your life too is in danger.'

'Mine? Is someone trying to kill me then?' I asked lightly.

'Perhaps. I would not take any chances of being found out in the open. There is a bad moon rising, the stars are unfavourable and the wind is blowing change.'

'Are you a fortune teller then?' I asked.

'You can choose not to believe me,' he said gently. 'But I gather most of my news from the wind itself. Today news came to me of a wandering goddess and of her husband, camped not two days' march away. If he hurries, he will be here late tomorrow night. But for Hephaestion the wind is blowing bitterly. I cannot imagine him getting much older.' His voice was sorrowful. His eyes held mine.

'I must see Bagoas,' I whispered.

'Impossible.'

'No, nothing is ever impossible.' I thought a minute. 'Which god does he worship?'

'He worships Ea, in the largest temple by the river. He goes every morning as the first rays of the sun pierce the night. Would you speak to him?'

'No. I would kill him.' I was surprised at the coldness in my voice.

The man smiled and took my hand. 'You will listen to me. I am not very wise, nor rich, nor powerful, but the wind is my friend and he speaks to me. If he thought Bagoas would die he would have told me.'

'I didn't know until just now that he would die,' I said.

'Then I wish you luck.'

'You said you weren't rich, well, now you are.' I took a heavy purse from inside my robe and put it in his hands.

'There is enough gold there to make you and all your children rich.'

He gasped as he took it. There was a long silence as he searched for words. Finally he reached over and patted my arm shyly. 'The wind was right about you, at any rate. He said you were a treasure.'

'Which wind was it?'

He smiled. 'The West Wind. He says he knows you well.'

'Thank you.' I waved and left. He stared after me until I was out of sight. I felt lighter. The gold had been very heavy. I had given him a small fortune. Now I had to find Axiom and tell him what I planned to do. And Plexis had to know. So did Alexander.

# Chapter Eight

Four days after Alexander's arrival he came to see me. I was impatient, nearly out of my mind with worry and cross with everyone, even snapping at Chiron.

It was Chiron's birthday; Alexander used that excuse to come to see me. He gave him a wooden chariot with wheels that turned, pulled by two articulated horses.

The gifts Roxanne sent were burned. Axiom didn't even bother showing them to me; he knew by now what to look for. Roxanne's slave had given the gifts to Millis, and Axiom had snatched them right out of his hands and tossed them into the fire. Poor Millis didn't know what to think. He was unhappy with all the secretive undercurrents but I wouldn't tell him what was happening. I was still unsure of his loyalties. I was making him miserable, but it couldn't be helped. I was unhappy too, I hated living in the women's quarters, hated having to watch out for poison every moment, and I was frightened for my son.

When Alexander came to see me I burst into tears and threw myself into his arms.

'I can't live like this,' I sobbed. 'I'm so unhappy. Take me away from here, please.'

'Ashley!' He was shocked. 'You're so thin!'

'I can't eat. There's poison everywhere. I'm afraid for Chiron, and I'm afraid for you, and for Plexis.'

'What will happen to him? Do you know now?'

'I think so. Bagoas means to poison him.'

Alexander stiffened. 'Bagoas? That can't be!'

'It is true.' I dried my tears. 'I heard it from a reliable source.'

Alexander went very pale. The colour left his cheeks and he sat down suddenly. 'Bagoas? Poison? How?' His voice was strained.

'I have no idea,' I told him. 'But maybe we can kill Bagoas.'

'But, Ashley, if Hephaestion does not die *you* will be destroyed by your time gods.'

'They're not gods,' I said, suddenly angry.

'We can do nothing.'

'We can pretend he really did die,' I told him.

'Pretend? How?'

'Listen.' I told him the plan I'd formulated. There was a deep silence after I finished speaking that seemed to shake the walls. Or maybe it was just my pounding heart.

'Are you sure that will work?' he asked.

'It has to.'

'By the gods,' he said suddenly. Sweat trickled down his forehead. He wore a blank, stunned look. 'In three weeks, you say?'

'If I remember my ancient history right.'

He leaned over and put his head between his knees. 'Your ancient history is my future. I feel ill.'

'I've felt like that for a year now,' I told him. 'If you don't help me, I'll go mad. And please believe me, I could never spend my life as a Persian princess. I feel like I'm in prison. I miss being in the tent with you and seeing the sun rising in a different place nearly every morning. I'm like a bird that has been born in the wild and suddenly finds itself with its wings clipped in a cage.'

'A golden cage, but a cage just the same.'

'Even you will always be nothing but a tiger in chains if you stay. Didn't Opis teach you anything?'

'You heard about my speech? What did you think? Was it good? I made it up spontaneously. I was so mad I just shouted.' He sounded pleased.

'It was impressive.'

'Thank you.' He leaned over and kissed me. 'Oh, Ashley. Do you remember when I told you I missed floating in the river with you, swimming and hunting crocodile together?'

'Of course. I miss that too, except the part about the crocodiles.'

'I still miss that. We'll be free once more. I can't believe I'm saying this, but I swear to you, we'll be free once more.'

'Thank you, Alex.'

'Now I just have to kill Bagoas, tell Plexis to pretend to die, and nearly die myself before being saved by you. Compared to that, conquering Persia was like falling off a wild ass.'

'Ah. Another Macedonian saying? I thought you said you liked a challenge?' I teased.

'I said that? I'll have to start watching what I say in front of you, you have a habit of throwing things back at me.'

I was smiling. 'Please don't let me down,' I said.

'I won't. I promise.'

I drew a long, shaky breath. He had said it. He had finally said it. Now everything was in the hands of the gods. Hopefully, the gods would give *me* a helping hand.

Plexis played polo as he rode; naturally. As if it were no more difficult than breathing. His horses seemed as much a part of him as his legs or arms. He was a centaur. That's what most people were saying as they watched the new satrap of Ecbatana riding his horse back to the pony lines to change mounts.

His team was winning; they'd won all the matches so far. Plexis was in his element. Far from the palace and its court, he became what he was meant to be. Alexander watched from his throne and there was the saddest look in his eyes, as if he had realized just to what prison he had condemned his friend. Not that he'd ever complained. Plexis bent to his task as seriously as he could. His face lost its puckish good humour and took on a determined look. He stopped going to the stables every free minute and shut himself in his office with the scribes and accountants. Yet his fervour did him more harm than good.

In going over the accounts he discovered a grave error that seemed to indicate that some of the men Alexander had left to rule the cities of Persia and Greece had been embezzling. There was an investigation, and in a very short time Alexander had arrested seven men for misappropriation. He had them executed, which pleased some, but not all, of his generals. One of the men,

Cleander, had been Coenus's own brother. Now some whispered that Coenus had been killed by Alexander for speaking up when we'd reached the Beas river, telling Alexander that the army wanted to go no further. That was ridiculous, of course but it was true that Alexander had ordered the investigation of the men convicted of embezzling. He hadn't taken part in their trials but he had approved the sentence. The thunder on the horizon was growing louder.

Alexander seemed deaf to its warnings. True to character, not a subtle bone in his magnificent body, his eyes flashing, he stood firmly on the throne of Persia. In his speeches, he told everyone that he wanted his kingdom to be a jewel on the face of the earth. He expected everyone to obey his satraps, because he chose them for their loyalty and their talent. He said he expected to go on another long voyage, this time to the deepest part of Africa, where he would bring back riches undreamed of for the kingdom. It was your usual kingly speech but there was also the usual grumbling. Some people are never happy.

'I tried to tell you,' I told Alexander, holding his head on my lap and stroking his forehead. 'In my time all the countries have splintered. There is a phenomenon where one man sweeps in and creates a huge kingdom. Then the man disappears and the natural opposing forces break everything apart. It takes an exceptional man to bring so many different people together. When you disappear there will be a vacuum. It is more human, I think, to be individuals.

'We are *too* individual,' I added, thoughtfully. 'We have split into smaller and smaller factions. In my time, there are more than twenty-five countries where you have made but one. Amazing, isn't it? And even those countries threaten to split off and form smaller ones. In a few centuries maybe a conqueror will come and reunite them again. So far the only one to do it was you. My handsome warrior.' I kissed him on the mouth and then popped a grape into it.

He chewed lazily. The sun was at its hottest. The polo games would resume in the evening. Plexis had not been offered anything to drink by anyone suspicious. Bagoas remained hidden. Alexander had tried to see him, but he was not in his quarters.

'Another one?' He opened his mouth like a baby bird.

'You're too spoiled,' I sighed.

'Mmm, that was a good grape.' He swallowed and opened his mouth. 'Again.'

'You're worse than Chiron.'

'Have you weaned him yet?'

'He's three years old! He's been weaned for nearly a year now.'

He leered at my breasts. 'Too bad, I would have liked some ...'

There was a knock at the door and a voice called to Alexander. It was the guard. He said something about the game starting again.

'So soon?' I asked. 'It's still hot out.'

'Plexis wants to finish early; he has to oversee the

festivities this evening. He's taking this satrap business seriously.' Alexander got to his feet in a fluid movement and pulled me up beside him. 'I'll see you after the game,' he whispered.

'See you later, alligator,' I said.

'In a smile, crocodile.' Well, he was learning.


I had no intention of waiting like a good little wife in the gynaeceum. I put on my men's clothes and wig. Axiom and Brazza kept Chiron, as usual, but they were not happy about my going to the games alone.

'It's too dangerous, there are too many rough men. And there are soldiers who could recognize you.'

'No they won't, I'll stay hidden. Don't be such a worry-wart.'

Axiom had no idea what *that* could be, but his narrow face darkened. 'Please, my lady, at least take Millis with you.'

'I can't! Everyone knows he's my slave. They'll recognize me for sure.'

'Not if he wears a disguise.'

Millis looked swarthy and almost dangerous with the black wig Axiom gave him. I put some charcoal on his cheeks and darkened his eyebrows. Then we both crept out the window. He was so thrilled I trusted him at last that he made me feel beastly for not telling him before. He couldn't stop grinning and patting me on the shoulder.

As we made our way down the narrow streets towards the wide avenues, I told him what was happening. His expression became serious. He explained with gestures that he would defend me with his life, and I stood on tiptoes and kissed him. It must have looked funny; a thin youth carrying a short staff kissing a menacing thug. Millis grinned. I'd blackened one of his teeth as well. His mother wouldn't have recognized him.

At the polo game, we squeezed into the crowd. Everyone in Ecbatana seemed to be there; men, children, and women, the rich and the poor. Everyone was shouting or cheering. Most of them were eating or drinking. There were kebab vendors, men selling dried fruit and pistachios, stands with slices of watermelon and piles of dates, vats of mead and beer, and people hawking commemorative plates and cups with Alexander's face painted on them. I was caught up in the din and hurly burly and almost forgot why we were there, but then I caught sight of the polo field and my good mood vanished.

We found a space in the stands and settled down to watch the match. I saw Alexander on the far side of the field. Of course, we couldn't get anywhere near him. He was protected by his soldiers. There was a large empty space around him. We were directly opposite the royal throne.

I'll never know what made him look up and see me. He always knew when I was looking at him. He told me that he could actually feel my eyes upon him, like a cool touch. Whatever it was, I saw him looking in my direction and I waved. It wasn't an odd gesture to make – everyone was waving. I saw him blench though. His fingers whitened on the arms of his throne and he leaned forward. Nobody noticed except me. He didn't wave back. That would have condemned me to death. He turned his head. The game was getting under way. A hush fell over the crowd, and I tightened my grip on my staff.

There are poisons, and there are poisons. Some worked on men, and some on horses.

As we watched, the horse Plexis was riding suddenly died. He didn't slow or stagger, he collapsed while at full gallop. Plexis was thrown and the horse rolled over him. After the crash, there was a moment when everyone held their breath. Then Alexander vaulted over the barrier and rushed out to the field while a general flood of humanity surged forward to get a better look.

I fought through the crowd, making my way to the field. I was demented, nothing could stop me from clawing a path to Plexis. Millis helped. He was big and brawny and shoved people right and left.

Plexis was lying in an awkward sprawl, his neck twisted sideways, blood seeping from his mouth and nose. I threw myself down at his side. He was still breathing, but the sound he made as he struggled for air was awful. I called his name and his eyelids fluttered, but there was no other sign he was conscious. Alexander was standing over him, keeping the crowd at bay. His soldiers had been slower to react and they were just now forcing the people back. I raised my eyes and met Alexander's gaze.

'Make sure nobody moves him until Usse gets here, then bring him to my quarters,' I said clearly. I waited until he whispered, 'All right'. Then I wriggled out of the crowd and found Millis. 'Quick, take me to the temple of Ea,' I said. I held something in my hand that looked like a staff but wasn't. Millis knew what it was, but he did as I asked.

Bagoas was in the temple. He had been there for days, making sure he had an alibi. Perhaps he felt safe there. He knew that Alexander would kill him if he suspected he had a hand in Hephaestion's death. He hadn't counted on me.

He was a medium-sized, slender man. His hair was dyed brassy blond, and his eyes were velvety black with long lashes. The whites of his eyes were very pure, and his eyebrows were delicately arched. His brow was high and clear. His skin was incredible. It was like ivory satin. He had a faint pink flush on his cheeks. He was beautiful. A deadly cherub.

He watched me enter the temple. His eyes were wide and brilliant. His full and sensuous mouth curved in a smile. He rose from where he had been kneeling and walked towards me. He was so light on his feet he looked as if he were dancing. He wore nothing but a golden chain around his neck, and a short pleated linen skirt.

I had lost my wig, and my cropped hair must have shone like silver in the dark temple. My face felt strangely stiff. My skin was cold. I couldn't feel my hands or feet. Shock was flowing like ice through my veins.

Bagoas lowered his chin, studying me. His mouth opened, and the tip of his pink tongue came out and touched his upper lip. I felt my nipples harden as my body responded to his sexuality. His whole presence was a beautiful invitation to lust.

'Come, child,' he said in a seductive lilting voice. 'What is your name?'

'Nemesis,' I said clearly. Then I lifted the short spear

that Barsine had given me so very long ago in Persepolis, and, with both hands, I drove it through his chest.

He fell backwards, gasping and clawing at the shaft of my spear, but I held on. Then Millis grabbed the end of it, adding his weight, and I felt the tip of the spear hit the stone floor. Swallowing my sudden nausea, I bent over and whispered into Bagoas's ear. 'What did you do to Hephaestion?'

'Poison,' he said. 'Is he dead?' His voice was fading.

'No, but you are,' I said. Then I wrenched the spear free and left. The priests in the temple made no move to stop me.

# Chapter Nine

Bagoas died in the temple. There was an inquiry. The priests said a blond youth called Nemesis and a tall man with missing teeth had entered the temple and struck Bagoas down. They also mentioned poison. Eumenes, Alexander's secretary, in writing the news to Athens, made it sound as if Bagoas had died of poison.

Usse transported Plexis to my quarters, as I had asked, and Alexander went insane with grief. I caught a glimpse of the dark folly that would consume him when his friend died.

According to Usse, the fall had broken one of Plexis's arms, his thorax had been compressed, he'd displaced and cracked a vertebra in his neck, and his head, unprotected, had hit the ground. He was in a coma. He wavered between waking and sleep. No one was allowed into my quarters to see him, except Usse and Alexander. Everyone accepted this arrangement. I was a goddess. Naturally Alexander would trust his best friend's life with me.

One week after the fall, Usse formally announced Hephaestion's death. His new wife, Drypetis, already fragile, was so shocked she lost her baby. She hadn't come to see her husband once. I think part of the shock came from knowing he was with me, in my quarters, and that I had forbade anyone to see him. Except Drypetis. I'd sent a message to her right away, telling her to come immediately. I was hoping she'd refuse. It turned out I'd judged her harshly, but well. She sent a message back saying she'd rather die than set foot in my rooms. She then demanded to have him sent to her rooms. I refused. Three days after his death was announced, she lost her child. I felt the loss like a blow. I hadn't wanted that to happen. I was afraid to say anything to Plexis, and he didn't know for a very long time. The secret was a heavy burden of guilt for me.

Alexander went into a frenzy of mourning. He ordered all the cavalry horses' manes and tails cut short. He chopped off his own hair and locked himself in my quarters for two days. No one could see him. Stories of his wild grief circulated. People shook their heads and clucked sympathetically. When I was sure that everyone was starting to compare his grief with that of Achilles for his friend Patroclus, I was ready to carry out my plan.

Alexander ordered a huge funeral cortège that would carry Hephaestion to Babylon, where a monument was to be erected in his honour. He wrote a letter to the temple of Amon in Egypt asking if he should honour his friend as a god, or as a hero.

'A *god or a hero*?' Alexander frowned at the letter he was writing and looked back at me. 'I did that?'

'In the history books it says you went batshit crazy,' I said. I was sitting next to Plexis. He was still critical but he'd slowly started to recover. Two things had saved him. The rain that had fallen the night before, soaking the polo ground and making it soft, and the fact that I had told

113

Alexander not to move him until Usse got there. He had a badly cracked vertebra in his neck. He would have to remain absolutely still for at least six months. The prospect was making him cranky, to say the least. He had also drunk out of his own wine flask just before the game, but the poison inside it didn't kill him. Usse had given him a massive dose of charcoal, but his stomach pained him for a long time afterwards.

'What does "went batshit" mean?' asked Alexander, applying himself to his letter. Near the doorway, Millis and Axiom were wailing and carrying on, making the people gathered outside believe we were all mad with sorrow. Letters of condolence arrived from all over the kingdom. Millis took them and put them in a large chest. Eumenes would take care of them. Meanwhile, we had to hide Plexis. What better place to hide him than in my own quarters? To Axiom, Brazza, and Millis we had explained that we were telling everyone that Plexis was dead because he had many enemies and we wanted to save his life.

Axiom and Brazza had accepted everything we'd said with no questions. I was worried about trusting Millis, but so far he had proved himself very useful. Usse was harder to convince, but for now he held his tongue.

'Batshit means what it sounds like, but batshit *crazy* means you went beyond normal crazy.' I smoothed a lock of hair from Plexis's brow. 'How are you feeling today?' I asked him softly.

He frowned. 'Fuzzy. Usse gives me the strangest potions.'

'You can't move at all. Did you understand everything

Usse told you?' I asked.

'Yes, I did. I also remember what you told me. I have to stay inside my own mausoleum for a whole year?'

'No, not quite. Usse will tell you when it's safe for you to move. But you very nearly died.'

'Of poison and a riding accident, amazing. So I stay perfectly still until next spring. It's going to be very lonely without you both.'

'I know. I'm sorry. If you want to stop this whole silly charade just tell me, and I'll give you the rest of the poison.'

He widened his eyes. 'I simply said I'd miss you!'

'I'm sorry, I didn't mean to frighten you. Besides, you won't be alone.'

'That's all right. Now that I'm on my deathbed it's time to fulfil the prophecy and answer all my questions.' He sounded smug, but there was a faint waver in his voice. He was far from well.

I leaned over and kissed him lightly. 'Ask if you dare, Plexis. I might even tell you.'

'Did you really kill Bagoas?'

It made me sick to think about it. Even though it had been premeditated, and I'd practised driving a spear through a side of mutton, I never would have done it if I hadn't seen Plexis in agony on the polo field. 'I didn't think I could ever kill a human being,' I said. 'But I was infuriated. Bagoas was a monster.' I paused. There was something I had wanted to ask Alexander. 'Is it true that Bagoas tried to seduce you?'

He looked surprised. 'Where did you hear that?'

My eyes narrowed. 'Let's just say I heard it. How on earth did you resist?'

'Who said I resisted?'

'I heard that you'd refused him, and that he wanted to be satrap of Ecbatana, and that's why he was so angry at you he wanted to kill Plexis.'

Alexander tilted his head. 'You saw him, didn't you? Do you think anyone could resist him? Of course I didn't refuse. By the gods, woman, just thinking about him makes me hard. But he wanted something else, and I wouldn't give it to him.'

'What did he want?'

'He wanted to be appointed satrap in Babylon, not Ecbatana.' He shook his head. 'He was made for love, not ruling; it's true what you said about him. In some ways he was monstrous and he frightened me.'

'How did you know about the poison in my wine flask?' Plexis spoke up weakly.

I touched his cheek gently. 'That was Millis. He pointed out Bagoas's slave-boy at the polo game. He was standing near your horse. He was acting as a groom, but you'd left your wine flask unattended. It was easy for him to slip some poison into it.'

'And what happened to the slave-boy?' His voice was fading fast.

'Alexander had him crucified,' I said matter-of-factly. 'Along with the man who'd made the poison. Then he razed the temple of Ea, where Bagoas died. The man who made the poison knew what he was doing,' I continued, anticipating his next question. 'He was a doctor, someone named Glaucias.'

'By Zeus.' Plexis whispered. Then he closed his eyes and fell asleep in an instant. His breathing was clear, not the sonorous sound of a coma. I felt my shoulders relax and I slumped wearily on the bench.

Alexander finished his letter and sealed it. 'I do feel rather silly doing this. Are you sure the history books say I "went batshit crazy"?'

'They don't say that,' I said teasingly. 'They say you lay on your friend's body for days, crying, and that you cut all the horse's manes and tails off.'

'Well, I did that, now what?'

'Did you give orders for the funeral cortège? We're going to have to be very careful; he's still not out of the woods.'

'He's in a palace, not in the forest,' said Alexander.

'Sorry, it's another expression. It means he's not well yet. When he's transported, he has to be perfectly still. He'll die if he's jolted. We won't be able to relax until he's hidden in Babylon. Are you sure he'll be well hidden in the palace?'

'You gave me the idea. He'll be safe in your rooms. You'll be hugely pregnant then; no one will dare enter your rooms. I'll make sure of that.'

'I was *never* hugely pregnant,' I said indignantly.

'Well, hippopotamusly pregnant then.'

'That's not a word,' I said, giggling.

'Don't laugh, someone might hear you.' He stood up and moved to Plexis's side. He reached down and touched his hair, softly. 'I can't believe I almost lost him.' He knelt at Plexis's bedside and stared at his friend's bruised face. 'He looks so ill,' he said.

'He's still in danger,' said Usse gravely.

'What else did the history books say I did?' asked Alexander.

'I think you went north and slaughtered some poor tribe in the Zagros Mountains.'

'What? Artabazus's tribe?' He was incredulous.

'A historian named Plutarch said so.'

'Where is this fellow? I never heard of a Plutarch among my scribes and historians.'

'He's not born yet. I think he's born in the year 50 AD. I'm not quite sure though.'

'And just when exactly *is* 50 AD?' Alexander looked perplexed, as well he might.

'In around four hundred years.'

'Do you mean to say the only information you have about me was written four hundred years from now? Do you realize how stories can change in that much time? What happened to all the reports written by my scribes and historians?'

'This is going to be a long story,' I told him. 'You had best sit down. Or we can talk about it some other time.'

'Some other time.' Alexander sighed. 'So, now I have to storm into the Zagros and slaughter Artabazus's tribe?'

'I said I wasn't sure. Why don't you just issue a vague warning to anyone up north telling them not to consider treason or you'll get really mad and let Onesicritus handle the rest. If you let him, he'll write back to Athens telling them you've razed Persia.'

'And wouldn't they just love that.' He sighed. 'All right, that sounds reasonable.'

Plexis opened his eyes again. They were dark with pain. His sleep never lasted long. Luckily Usse was not far and we called him. He bent over his patient, giving him some more medicine, and taking his pulse. 'Greetings from the world of Hades,' said Plexis. His voice was just above a whisper.

'Hang on,' I said.

Plexis's eyes searched for Alexander's face. 'Are you still organizing things? I can't believe I'm assisting in my own funeral plans. They seem a bit outrageous, to say the least. I never knew you cared so much.' Tears leaked out of the corners of his eyes and Alexander leaned over and brushed them away with his fingertips.

'It's Ashley, she's telling me what I should do. Believe me, I never would have thought of all this myself. A mausoleum three stories tall with life-size horses on it made of straw, can you imagine? Not to mention the peacocks, eagles, archers with golden bows, and the whole thing made to resemble a giant ship.'

'What's so strange about that?' He grinned. 'Nearchus will be so happy. Ouch. It hurts when I laugh.'

'Don't. I'm beginning to think that Ashley doesn't really remember anything, and she's just telling me these things to make me look ridiculous to future generations. Not to mention what my generals will think. I'm glad Nearchus's not here …' His voice trailed off as he saw his friend's face. 'What is it? Plexis! Are you all right?'

'What do you mean, Ashley remembers? How can you

119

remember something that hasn't happened yet?' His face was ashen and I grew frightened. Shock would certainly kill him.

'Plexis,' Alexander's voice was gentle. 'You're not afraid are you? You? The only one brave enough to jump off the roof of the consul's house in Pella that summer when you came to visit?'

'I broke my leg, if you remember correctly,' said Plexis.

'I didn't say you were smart, I said you were brave. Plexis, Ashley can remember what hasn't happened because she comes from the future. It's as simple as that. Plexis? Plexis?' He looked at me worriedly. 'Did he faint?'

I called Usse and the doctor came running. He looked at Plexis and shook his head. 'No, it's just the potion. He's sleeping normally. Don't worry. Try to rest now, my lady. You're too thin. I keep telling you that.'

My mouth twitched. 'I know, but tell that to my husband. He's already comparing me to a hippopotamus.'

Usse stood by silently. I'd killed Bagoas, Usse had heard about that. Then we'd told everyone Plexis had died. We'd known about the poison in the wine. We'd given the slave-boy some of it and he'd died in agony. Then Alexander had crucified his body as a warning to anyone else who wanted to try poison. Now Usse watched us, his expression worried. He was wondering what was happening. I wanted to tell him everything, but it was taking me a long time to weigh the consequences.

Alexander went to the Zagros Mountains and came

120

back two weeks later. He told me he'd seen his son, Heracles, and that he was a strong, seven-year-old boy with red-gold hair and grey eyes.

'Artabazus and his wife dote on him. He's a happy, healthy child. I told Artabazus that I wouldn't ever declare him my heir, and that if I were to die he was to take the boy to their borderlands in the north and hide him until it was safe.'

'That was a brave thing to do.' I stroked his head and held it to my breast.

Alexander had been gloomy ever since he'd come back. Seeing his son was just part of it. He'd had time to think about his own childhood, something he hated to do.

'I wanted to bring him here but I've started to see that there is too much danger. When I was growing up I didn't think about what was really happening.' He shuddered against me. 'I had eleven brothers and sisters. Only four are alive today: Nike, Ptolemy, Arrhidaeus, and Cleopatra. And Cleopatra isn't really related to me, she was one of my father's concubine's daughters. All the other children died of poison. Arrhidaeus nearly died, and now he's a complete idiot.' His voice was strained.

'I'm sorry,' I said.

'So am I. In your time, do such things happen?'

'No, not exactly. There are still murderers, but we don't have any absolute rulers. The whole world has become a democracy. Well, nearly all the world.'

'That must be nice. That's what I always wanted my kingdom to be.' Alexander reached up and touched my shorn head. 'Why did you have to cut your hair?' he asked.

'Because I wanted to save Plexis.'

'He's still very sick.'

'We're going to have to go very slowly all the way to Babylon.'

'Don't worry,' he said,' I'll take care of him.'

'I'm not worried, who's worried?' I looked down at my husband, sprawled across my lap. 'It's just that time is suddenly leaping forward. It's February already. Plexis has been hidden in my quarters for two months already. I'm impatient to go to Babylon and find Paul.'

'And I die in the late spring.'

'Alex?'

'Mmm?'

'Where shall we go first?'

'After you save me?' He looked amused. 'We'll head in whichever direction you want to go, north, south, east, or west. We'll take my tent, an elephant, and some horses, Axiom, Brazza, Usse, Plexis, and the children.'

'And everything will be as it was. We'll swim in the rivers, lie in the sun, fight crocodiles, and be happy ever after.'

'May the gods hear you,' said Alexander. But he stared past me out the window, and a worried frown marred his brow. He was watching the builders make the final touches to Plexis's funeral monument.


When the monument to Hephaestion was finished, we had a ceremony to put Plexis in his final resting place. We wrapped him up in linen, like a mummy, and carefully placed him in a gilded coffin painted with horses. Usse,

Millis, Axiom, and Alexander carried him slowly to the special, lavishly furnished room built to hold his remains. The whole court lined up to say farewell. I insisted on holding the ceremony at night, so that no one could see that Usse slipped inside. Poor Usse! He would take care of Plexis for the journey, and he would only be able to leave the mausoleum at night.

The travelling mausoleum was like a three story parade float in the shape of a giant ship. Standing on the deck were thirty-two life-sized horses made of straw, one for each year of Plexis's life. Each horse wore a scarlet silk blanket embroidered in gold with a huge letter "H" for Hephaestion. Egret plumes, peacock feathers, and silver bells completed the ornamentation. On the next level, fifty life-sized archers holding golden bows knelt among stuffed peacocks. One hundred and twenty eagles made of gold garnished the last level. The monument creaked along on sixteen wooden wheels, and it was pulled by twenty white oxen.

'Are you *sure* about this?' Alexander asked worriedly, staring at the wheeled wonder.

"Oh yes,' I said, trying desperately to remember what Hephaestion's mausoleum was supposed to look like. All I could recall was that it had been ostentatious. "I think there may have been one more level.'

'It won't fit under the gates of the city. What do your history books say I do with it? Do we burn it outside?'

'No, I think you have to knock down a wall.'

From inside the mausoleum, came the sound of hysterical laughter. Alexander pounded on the wood. 'Be quiet in there. You're supposed to be dead.'

> *"How many miles to Babylon?*
> *Three score and ten.*
> *Can I get there by candlelight?*
> *Yes, and back again.*
> *If your heels are nimble and light,*
> *You may get there by candlelight."*

I lost track of the number of times I sang that ancient song. Ancient song? Only to me. To the others, it was new and unusual. I taught it in English so that it sounded like great incantations, like the *Row, Row, Row Your Boat* song we'd sung with the soldiers on the Indus River.

Actually, I was trying to keep Chiron entertained. For a small boy, travelling long distances in cramped quarters was unbearable. Whenever we could, we'd leave the curtained wagon and play outside. When that happened, the Persian guards would turn their backs – afraid to look upon me. These were the same men who had been with us during the trek across Asia, who'd ridden with me, swam with me, joked with me – but now that Alexander was officially king of Persia, I was a Persian queen, and taboo. The Greek and Macedonian men were affronted. How dare the Persians treat me so rudely?

I didn't get involved. I was afraid of starting futile arguments. Both sides were convinced the other was about to be struck down by the bloodthirsty gods of etiquette, I suppose. Therefore, I didn't go outside much. The voyage was wearing on all our nerves.

When Plexis had a particularly bad day we had to stay

one or two days without moving him.

Alexander would give orders not to disturb him, and he would stay all day in his tent. Eumenes, his secretary, wanted to write everything down, but the delays and slow pace were difficult to explain. Usually Alexander covered fifty kilometres a day with his army. Now we were barely inching along.

Near Babylon, Plexis took a turn for the better and we were able to pick up the pace. It was a great relief to Eumenes, who, mindful of Alexander's orders, had been writing things like, *'on the fifth day of the month he drank and on the sixth and seventh days he rested ...'* Not the sort of thing he wanted to write for posterity.

We were all very nice to Eumenes. I thought he was a pleasant change from Onesicritus and I liked talking to him. Unfortunately, I wasn't free to talk to anyone. We were still in Persia, still following the Persian laws of protocol, and I was off-limits to anyone but Alexander and the women of my court. Since I had no women with me, my company consisted of Alexander and Brazza. Luckily, we got lots of mail, so I usually had things to read. Sis sent us messages daily from Ecbatana, and from Bablylon came news from Nearchus.

One day he sent news that Paul had arrived in Babylon. I was relieved and frantic with worry at the same time. Nearchus had said he would guard Paul, and I trusted him. But in the same letter, he said that Olympias had arrived in Babylon as well.

'What in Hades' name is your mother doing there?' I cried, waving my arms.

'How should I know? By the gods, woman, do I look like an oracle?' Alexander ran a nervous hand through his hair making it stick up in spiky cow-licks.

'It's going to make things very difficult,' I said. 'She has spies everywhere.'

'Just let her try to spy on me,' he said darkly.

'All right, she's in Babylon, and there's nothing to be done about it. Just do something for me, tell her that my quarters are absolutely out of bounds to everyone, including my dear mother-in-law.' I stomped my foot.

'She'll want to see the children,' he said apologetically.

'The hell she will!' I exploded.

He winced. When I spoke in English, it meant I was losing my temper. 'I'll deal with her. Just let me take care of everything. I'll put you in the garden palace, and that way I can put the royal guard around your quarters.'

'And where will *you* stay?' I asked bitterly.

'Don't look at me like that. I'll stay with you, of course. But officially I'll be in the Grand Palace.'

I sat on the bed and glared at him. 'I'll look at you any way I want.' My brows drew together in a frown.

Alexander sat by my side and pulled me to him. 'I'm sorry, Ashley. I know what you're thinking. But I promise, when I'm in Babylon I won't make love with my other wives, not even once. All right?'

I pushed him away as if I'd been stung. 'Is that why you think I'm mad? Let me tell you something, Buster, if you dare to make love with one of your other wives while we're in Babylon I will personally make sure history happens just exactly as it's written. In other words, if you

126

value your life, don't even think about it.'

He looked amused. 'That's not what's bothering you? Then what is?'

'You are incredible!' I shrieked, springing to my feet and waving my arms. 'I'm about to be locked up in a cage and all you can say is, "don't worry, I won't make love to my other wives"?' Very reassuring. I want to be free, damn it!'

Alexander lost his smile. 'Is that all?' he asked bleakly.

I was startled by his change of mood. 'Why, yes,' I said, frowning.

'Because, you *are* free, you know. Whenever you want, you can go. You can take Plexis, Axiom, Usse, Brazza even, and go wherever you want to. I'll never stop you. If you're unhappy with me, I will not keep you. If I knew of a way to send you back to your time I would, if you wished that. There are some days when I feel terrible for kidnapping you. I had no way of knowing the consequences, and now I am sorry.'

I sat down again and sighed. 'No, Alex, don't be sorry. I'm happy when we're together. The problem is, I hardly see you . You're gone from sunrise to sunset; you have a hundred things to do every day. Your life is no longer your own, and it has nothing to do with me. It's as if I've ceased to exist for you.'

There was a deep silence while he thought about this. Then he took my chin his hands and kissed me. I felt my bones dissolving. He kissed with the single-mindedness that marked all his actions. My arms crept around his neck and I pulled him to me. His hands slipped under my tunic and found my breasts. He weighed them in his hands, his thumbs stroking my nipples then he bent his head and suckled, pulling hard. I put my head on his shoulder and moaned softly. We lay back on the bed and Alexander finished taking off my clothes. He was naked beneath his skirt so all I had to do was untie his belt.

I nibbled his ear. 'I have a feeling you're trying to avoid talking to me,' I whispered.

'I'm trying to prove you exist,' he said. Then he slipped his hand between my legs, and I felt him smile against my cheek. 'And I've a feeling that you don't mind at all,' he chuckled.

I arched my back and gasped. He was right anyway, about that.

# Chapter Ten

We arrived in Babylon at sunrise next day. As we approached over the flat plain, I remembered my first sight of the fabled city nearly a decade before. I'd been riding an exhausted horse, drumming my heels into its lathered sides to urge it on. Paul, just an infant, had been earmarked for human sacrifice, and I had been desperate to save him. But Darius had reached him first, kidnapping him.

Olympias had wanted to sacrifice Paul. Her oracles had told her that Marduk, a bloodthirsty god, needed to drink Paul's blood. She hadn't told Alexander about Paul being his son. I had, though. Alexander had become violently enraged. Thankfully, I'd managed to persuade him not to kill his mother, and to pursue Darius to try to recover Paul. History stayed on track. The Time Senders weren't alerted.

Now, Olympias and Paul were in the same city, and I had no way of knowing if she'd given up trying to kill him. According to Alexander, she was dreadfully sorry and would never dream of harming her grandchild. Her excuse was that the stars had foretold the boy was the son of the crocodile god, not Alexander's son. She believed what the stars told her.

The stars were aligning. Spring was coming, and along with it, Alexander's death. But at the moment, my first concern was for Paul.

Soldiers arrived to accompany the funeral cortège. Alexander ordered a litter for me, so that I could go directly to Paul. He knew how much this meant to me. Just outside the city's walls, a large group of Alexander's soldiers and generals waited for us. As we approached, the Persians prostrated themselves. The Greeks and Macedonians stood stiffly, their arms raised in a military salute. They no longer mingled, I noted. But all that was pushed to the back of my mind when I saw my son. I spotted his bright gold head as soon as we arrived at the huge, blue gate of Ishtar. As promised, Nearchus was at his side watching over him.

When the litter was set on the ground, I clambered out and ran to Paul. He was tall and slender, his head level with my shoulders. We were laughing and crying as we hugged.

'Mommy! Mommy!' he cried, 'I missed you so much!'

'Oh, Paul, I missed you too. You've grown tall, let me look at you.' I held him away from me but my eyes were so full of tears I could see nothing but a blur. He stared back at me with that solemn look I remembered so well. 'Paul,' I whispered. 'My son, I'm so happy you're here.'

'Me too,' he said quietly, his voice wavering. I hugged him. My chest was tight with emotion but this was not the time or the place to cry. Hurriedly I wiped my face with the sleeve of my dress, straightened, and gazed around. The crowd was chanting Alexander's name, but the noise was just beginning to register.

Nearchus stood next to us. I wanted to give him a grateful hug as well but, mindful of the new protocol, I said, 'Thank you for keeping my son safe.'

We looked at each other, Alexander, Nearchus, Paul, and I; then Alexander gave a small nod. 'Are you ready?' he asked us. I tightened my hand on Paul's shoulders. The soldiers threw open the gates. We walked into Babylon.

Olympias had organized a huge welcome. A platform had been set up just inside the gate, and as we arrived trumpets blared and the people cheered and pelted us with flowers. We were deafened by the noise. Alexander looked at me, worried. He wanted to sneak Plexis into my quarters, but now he would have to wait until night fell. We had to salute the waiting crowd. Alexander had to make a long speech. And Olympias and I met for the first time.

I'd seen her before. When she'd come to the temple for Paul's sacrifice, I'd been hidden behind the tapestries in the temple. Her hair was apricot gold, her skin pearly, her brows finely arched, and her heavy-lidded eyes clear. She wore her favourite adornments: red coral earrings, a gold and coral necklace, and gold and coral bracelets. Although she was in Persia, she wore diaphanous robes that revealed her youthful silhouette. She was still beautiful. I still hated her.

'My Lady Persephone, Queen of Hades, Ashley of the Sacred Sandals, Demeter's Daughter, welcome to Babylon,' she said, giving me all my titles and bowing low.

'Olympias.' I stood stiffly next to Paul and held his hand tightly.

Olympias narrowed her eyes. I hadn't used a single one

131

of her titles. I looked around but didn't see Maia, Paul's nurse. I asked Olympias where the girl was.

She gave an indifferent shrug. 'She died. Paul has a new nurse. I chose her myself. She's better than the peasant woman. Maybe now Paul will start learning some manners.'

Alexander saved me from having to kill her. 'My wife is very tired and I will now take her to her quarters.'

'I prepared her rooms,' said Olympias.

'I gave orders to prepare the garden palace for both of us,' said Alexander, and for the first time Olympias looked scandalized.

'Your wife belongs in the women's quarters!' she cried.

'My wife will stay where I want her to stay.' Alexander's brows lowered and his eyes blazed. Olympias, who hadn't seen her son in over ten years, quailed.

'You have changed, my son,' she said slowly.

'For the better, I assure you.' His voice was pure ice.

'I am so sorry about Hephaestion,' she said to him. 'I know you cared for him deeply. His funeral monument is quite amazing. It must have been a painful reminder to see him all those years. He looked so like his brother Cxious.' She was quick. She went straight for the jugular. Now I knew what Alexander had suffered during his childhood.

Alexander didn't reply but a nerve started to twitch in his jaw. As Olympias opened her mouth to speak again he looked back out towards the cheering crowd and raised his arms above his head. The cheering redoubled. Olympias's voice was drowned out. Whatever she'd wanted to say went unheard.

We stood for a while so that the people could get a good look at their king, then we walked to the palace. Throngs of people lined the streets and they tossed flower petals at us as we walked by. Alexander and I held Paul's hand. I hoped that Axiom and Brazza were safely in our rooms with Chiron. Just before we reached the palace, Olympias leaned towards me.

'I will come to see my other grandson tomorrow.'

'No, I will bring him to you.' I said.

She stiffened, and then nodded. 'That will be fine.'

Alexander turned and faced his mother. 'No one is to go into my wife's quarters, under pain of death,' he said quietly.

Olympias looked at me from beneath lowered lashes. 'That's good,' she said.

I wondered what she meant by that.

Once I had settled in my quarters, Stateira summoned me to her rooms. I cursed under my breath as I dressed. I didn't particularly want to see her but, under Persian law, she was my queen, being Alexander's senior wife now that Barsine was dead.

I tried to feel charitable towards her; after all, she was in love with a man who had once described her as being, 'sweet as an adder and beautiful as a hippopotamus'. Stateira was not a great beauty. Calling her a hippo was mean though, but Alexander *had* been very young and he'd never loved her. She was not particularly nice to me.

It wouldn't be so bad, but when she summoned me I had to wait in the great hall in full view of everyone in the gynaeceum. The great hall was actually a long, two-storey roofed courtyard. The women's rooms were on the top floor, with a balcony that ran the length of the hallway. Roxanne leaned on her balcony and stared at me. She stared with no expression on her face, ignoring my smiles and little waves. *Very strange.* She and Stateira had become allies united against me. They spent most of their time together, weaving or ordering their slaves around. Just two, normal, Persian royal ladies. Except that one would have the other killed in very little time.

Poor doomed Stateira. She tried to make herself beautiful. She wore lots of make-up, Persian style. Her lips were carmine coated, her cheeks rouged, her heavy eyebrows plucked to surprised arches, and her eyes circled with black kohl and powdered lapis lazuli. She stuck her head over the balcony, saw me, and narrowed her eyes. I smiled cheerfully and waved. It had the unexpected effect of making her disappear. I frowned. When would she invite me to enter her apartments? She knew I was here now.

I sat in the garden hallway and waited. After another hour, I had to pee and I wondered what to do. A large potted palm tree was starting to look very much like a toilet. I crossed my legs tightly and cursed some more. Where was Stateira? I started feeling much less sorry for her fate. When I couldn't bear it any longer, I stood up, meaning to return to my quarters. That's when one of Stateira's slave girls came to get me and I recognized Chirpa. She had was the young slave girl that Alexander had given me. I'd given her to Stateira as a wedding present, on the condition she would be freed. However, I

134

saw Stateira hadn't done so. Chirpa still wore the copper bracelet around her upper arm that marked her a slave.

She bowed low before me.

'Don't you recognize me?' I asked her.

She turned cool, grey eyes towards me. 'Of course, my lady.'

'Does Stateira treat you well?'

She looked upwards at the balcony. I followed her gaze, and saw Stateira standing there, watching us. 'I will take you to the queen,' she said, discreetly putting her finger to her lips. I didn't try to speak to her again.

Stateira didn't stand when I entered to room. She was overdressed as usual. She wore a purple gown. Three metres of pearls were wrapped around her neck, and at least sixty mink had died to line her cloak. Her eyes looked like a racoon's with all the kohl she used. I bowed to her, not quite as low as she would have liked, then asked where the toilet was. She pointed to a large chamber pot in the corner of the room. An old eunuch stood next to it, fanning the air with a gilded palm-tree branch.

I sat down and relieved myself. It still felt odd going to the bathroom in front of everyone, even after all these years.

Stateira and I chatted for a few minutes, and then she dismissed me. That's it. Three sentences about the weather. A comment about my bulging belly and Stateira dismissed me like some vulgar rug salesman. I was furious. She'd made me wait an hour, knowing I was uncomfortable down there, and now I was dismissed? I gritted my teeth and bowed again. Then a slave showed me out.

135

I stormed into Alexander's room. He was studying a long, official-looking document and there were three generals sitting around him, Nearchus, Ptolemy Lagos, and Antipatros.

They looked at me sadly. Their hair was cut short, and I realized with shock that they were in mourning for Plexis.

The generals stood to greet me. Nearchus, who knew, perhaps more than anyone else, my feelings for Plexis, took my hand. 'My lady,' he said. 'How is Paul?'

'Fine, thank you, Nearchus,' I said. 'Alexander, can I talk to you alone for a second?'

'I'll be right with you,' he said. 'Go and wait in your quarters and I'll join you as soon as I'm done here.'

'What are you doing?' I asked, curious. My question made Ptolemy Lagos and Antipatros frown, but Nearchus answered me.

'We're planning a sea journey to Africa,' he said. 'I thought we could go to the south by a different route.' As always, when he was talking about boats or the sea, his voice rang with enthusiasm.

I smiled. 'That sounds like a wonderful idea.'

The other men were uncomfortable with me in the small room with them. As before, I was struck by the difference between travelling with them in the army and being in Persia, in the palace, under protocol rules. They were impatient for me to leave, so I did. I wandered back through the palace. Two mute eunuchs accompanied me through the maze of corridors. My feet made echoing sounds on the shiny tiles and my eyes feasted on the incredible frescos painted on the walls. I thought that the palace was very beautiful, and that I hated it. It was just a gilded cage. I cast a glance at my silent guards. They didn't dare look at me fully. They waited outside my quarters, like guard dogs, and whenever I stepped outside, they flanked me. We turned the last corner and I found myself in front of my heavy, wooden door. One guard rapped upon it and Axiom opened a little peep-hole and peered out. Seeing that it was me, he opened the door. Before I disappeared into my rooms, I turned and thanked my guards, asking them if they needed anything. They looked at a point just below my knees and nodded once, meaning 'No'. Then they turned and took their places beside the doorway. Nothing changed. I sighed and entered my quarters.

When Alexander came to my apartments two hours later, I was talking to Plexis. Chiron was napping, Paul was playing with a puzzle, and Axiom and Brazza were in town shopping. Millis was guarding Chiron.

'What did you want to see me about?' Alexander asked. He bent down and kissed Plexis.

'I wanted to tell you that I want you to take Chirpa away from Stateira and give her to me. Today. Right now.' I was still angry. 'I told you that Stateira was to free her.'

'Chirpa? Do you mean the girl who can tell if food is poisoned? Stateira didn't free her?' He looked up from his friend and frowned at me.

'No, she didn't. Are you listening to me? Stop kissing Plexis and talk to me!' I was exasperated.

'I'm listening.' He gave me an amused smile. 'I'll get

Chirpa back from Stateira, and you'll have a new slave to free. You're a strange woman, freeing all your slaves like that. It makes for interesting conversations with my generals.'

'I think it's a good idea.' Plexis spoke firmly.

'Do you really?' Alexander was sitting on the bench next to Plexis's bed and he leaned over and gave him a lingering kiss. 'By the gods, Plexis, when I think how close I came to losing you, I go mad.' His voice was soft.

'You "shit bats like crazy"?' Plexis grinned.

'I do.' He looked thoughtful. 'You've never asked about Drypetis.'

Plexis turned crimson. He looked at me and swallowed. 'I don't suppose I did. Perhaps if I still felt something for her, I would have. It was a short infatuation.'

'Ah, it was just a phase.' Alexander looked wise. Plexis raised his eyebrows, so he said airily, 'I'll explain some other time.' He stroked Plexis's cheek and kissed him again.

Plexis stirred restlessly, a thin smile on his face. 'Stop kissing me. Usse told me I mustn't move at all and you're making it difficult. Ashley is smarter. She keeps her hands to herself.'

Alexander pulled back. 'I'm sorry,' he said. 'I didn't mean to make you uncomfortable. Excuse me, I think I'll go see Stateira about getting Chirpa back.' He sounded contrite.

Plexis watched as Alexander left. He was pale from being inside for months and his eyes were feverish. Usse gave him some sort of tranquillizer to keep him immobile, but it didn't work for everything. There was a tell-tale bump under his thin muslin sheet.

Millis took care of Plexis's toilet and changed him. He was strong and deft. While I held his shoulders, to make sure that his neck stayed perfectly still, Millis would quickly do his job. At first Plexis had been mortified but, once, when he tried to move himself, the cracked bone pinched a nerve and the pain was so terrible he'd screamed and fainted.

Now he held still.

I patted his hand. 'Only one or two more months, then you'll be up and around,' I told him.

'I think I'll go mad long before then.' He closed his eyes and breathed deeply. On his cheeks was a faint blush. 'Do you think you could, you know, with your hands maybe?' He opened one eye and peered at me, his blush deepening. I could see his pulse pounding in the hollow of his throat.

The bump under the muslin was getting bigger.

I glanced towards the closed door. 'All right. But if you move, Usse will be furious.'

'I promise.' It was more of a sigh.

I used my hands and my mouth, and Plexis didn't move. He just trembled violently, and when it was over there was a sleepy half-smile on his lips.

'I think that I'll feel much better if you do that more often,' he said shyly. Only his voice was shy. There was a mischievous twinkle in his eyes.

I was so relieved to see him looking more like himself that I agreed. I also thought I'd ask Usse. I would hate to save Plexis and then be responsible for his demise.

Usse looked doubtful when I told him what I'd done, and he wondered if he shouldn't add something stronger to the potion that he was giving Plexis. But he decided against it when he saw how deeply Plexis was sleeping that afternoon.

Alexander became more haggard every day. Trying to create a government from what were essentially fighting factions was sapping his energy. But at least he could leave the palace. I wished I could too, as I'd done in Ecbatana, but I was getting too far along in my pregnancy. It would be difficult for me to disguise myself, unless it were as a hippo.

I missed the bustle and riot of the marketplace, and I started to understand Roxanne's fondness for the myriad slaves, ladies-in-waiting, squawking parrots, and screeching monkeys in her apartments. I loved my quiet rooms with their deep shade and their calm, but I longed to hear the bright chatter and shouts of people bargaining for goods, the minstrels' songs, and children's laughter as they rushed around the marketplace.

Actually, the royal palace in Babylon wasn't that bad. It was divided into several parts. Straddling the Euphrates, half of the palace was on one side of the river, and half on the other side. There was a narrow, covered bridge spanning the river for the royal women, and we could walk around the palaces as long as our eunuch guards accompanied us.

The hanging gardens were not in the women's part of

the palace. To get to them, we had to take the bridge and then underground hallways. The gardens were immense. They were built on staggered platforms. Water cascaded from one level to another and the sound was delicious. Tall date palm trees and ferns cast a fresh, green shade, and flowers grew in brilliant profusion.

Paul and Chiron loved to play in the gardens. Musicians, tourists, priests, merchants, and soldiers strolled through the wide, shady passages near the river. The gardens beckoned to everyone, and anyone could gain access to the main part of the gardens. Persian princesses and queens were cloistered, but I had persuaded Alexander to let me walk through the gardens as far as the outer gate. Although people would often stop and stare at me, everyone was friendly and polite. Paul and Chiron would run and shout, splashing their hands in the cool water, taking advantage of the green shade, their running footsteps echoing in the tiled corridors.

Outside the gardens, the white and rose walls of the city shimmered in the blinding heat. Inside, everything was cool and protected. During the hottest months of the year, merchants set up their stands in the echoing hallways.

I loved the gardens. My visual memories of Babylon are fading, except for the lapis blue and gold of the Ishtar Gate and the green tiles in my quarters. However, I can still see the long, shady corridors tiled with terracotta, pink pinpricks of sunlight on the floor like drops of blood. I can still recall the sound and the smell of the water running over brick aqueducts in the sun, splashing through the streams irrigating the hanging gardens. And the thick, verdant vegetation, redolent with jasmine, gardenia, and passion flower, will always stay with me.

Some days I would visit the women's palace. There was a swimming pool and another large garden just for the women. Their rooms looked onto a roofed courtyard, and their garden was just below. My rooms were not in the women's quarters, though. Alexander had a whole section of the smallest palace set aside for me and Plexis, who was now hidden in my bedroom. No one could come into my sanctuary, on pain of death. Alexander had made that quite clear.

My room was large and airy, with a garden all around it. Tall trees cast their shade onto the roof, keeping the rooms cool, and there was a swimming pool just outside my balcony.

Alexander was staying in the same palace as I was, to my immense relief. Normally he was expected to sleep in the Grand Palace, the one with the hanging gardens. That way, the king was near his administrators.

Stateira and Roxanne were both in the women's quarters with Olympias and Sis. Sis had left Drypetis in Ecbatana to be with her adored Alexander. However, the women were all very shocked about the sleeping arrangements, especially when Alexander refused to see his other wives at first. The priests started petitioning him; after all, he was their king and expected to make the crops grow and the sun rise and they were counting on him begetting at least one or two heirs to the crown. I had flatly refused to let anyone designate Paul or Chiron. Alexander didn't even acknowledge them as his official children. To appease the Persians, Alexander spent several nights with Stateira.

'Are you sure you're not jealous?' he asked me for the hundredth time.

I sighed and stared at him, my mouth a tight line. 'Of course I'm jealous. What do you expect? But I'm also a realist, and I know you don't care for her.'

'A realist?' his mouth quirked, then he was serious again. 'I don't care for her, but I feel guilty about it. Perhaps I'm only asking you to assuage my guilt.'

I blushed. There were a few things *I* felt badly about. I still hadn't spoken to Plexis about Drypetis. 'Maybe you are. I'm sorry, but I won't lie to you. When I think of you with Stateira it distresses me, but it's nothing I won't get over, all right?'

'It depends.'

'On what?'

'On how long it takes you to get over it.' He wasn't being facetious; he was quite earnest.

'Oh, it'll probably hurt until you come back and make love to me, then all will be forgotten,' I said, but my voice was sad and I couldn't manage a smile.

Alexander nodded, then turned to leave. Before he opened the door he looked at me over his shoulder and said, 'You know, all this is making it ridiculously easy to abdicate.'

He'd spoken so softy it was a moment before I understood him, and by the time I did, I was staring at an empty doorway.

Gifts arrived for my sons every day. I threw most of them away immediately. I was nervous and edgy about protecting the boys. Chiron was turning into a regular chatterbox, and I was terrified he'd say something about Plexis being in my room. Paul still had an unworldly sweetness about him. They had their own room next to mine, with Brazza, Millis, and Axiom caring for them. Olympias had tried to give me Paul's new nurse, but I was afraid she was a spy for my mother-in-law, so I'd sent her away.

However, Olympias insisted on seeing Paul and Chiron at least once a day, so I took them to her quarters myself and sat stiffly in her room while she tried to charm my boys. She always had sweets and little toys for them. I was not worried about poison coming from Olympias. She was besotted with her grandsons. I didn't worry about anything really, until she started to teach them about the Snake God and to tell them that their grandfather was actually Zeus-Amon. Chiron was too little to realize what she was saying but Paul's eyes widened.

'My grandfather was a snake?' he asked.

'No, dear, you're not paying attention. The great Zeus sometimes takes the form of a mighty serpent. I was sleeping one night with my beloved snakes when I felt something enter my vagina. It was Zeus as a snake and I ...'

'I think we've had enough excitement for one day,' I interrupted hurriedly, taking Chiron's arm and nodding to Paul. 'We'll see you tomorrow, Olympias.' I stepped over one of the harmless grass snakes Olympias kept as pets.

She had dozens of them slithering around her rooms. I didn't mind, and they certainly kept the insect population under control. Olympias had no ants, spiders, beetles, or mice in her quarters. She'd given Chiron and Paul each a little snake, and they kept them in wicker cages in their room.

'But I haven't finished telling them the story of their illustrious ancestry!' she cried.

'I think they've heard enough about their ancestry. Right now the children must eat.' I bowed. She waited until I was finished and bowed back, deeply. Then I bowed again, and she bowed —she was my husband's mother, and therefore my social superior, although she remained persuaded my mother was Demeter, which meant I was her superior, which made things confusing for both of us. After another round of bobbing, I left her rooms.

Paul tugged at my arm. 'How did grandmother know that snake was Zeus?' He had been paying attention after all.

I heaved a deep breath of relief when we were back in our own quarters. By the sundial, it was nearly noon. The boys would eat now, although after being stuffed with sweets they were never hungry for lunch. After Chiron's nap, I had to take the children to see Sis for an hour. She, too, insisted on seeing the children every day.

The two women couldn't be more different. Sis was a round, grandmotherly woman. She had grey hair and her face was full of friendly wrinkles. She always wore purple robes, befitting her rank. She was at least seventy, but her hands still moved quickly, with little, fluttery, butterfly movements when she talked, and she walked rapidly. I could hear her coming before I saw her. The long robes she wore trailed across the marble floors and the fringes of beads clicked with each quick step she took.

Olympias was languorous. Her arms were long and white. She moved slowly and majestically, even if she was just going to pee in the chamber pot. And when she did, she acted as if she was on stage; lifting up her dress bit by bit to bare her long white legs slowly, then she would carefully sit down, making sure everyone could see her shaved pubis. Even the eunuchs had erections when she was near.

I don't know how Olympias remained so beautiful. Her skin was like coral, the stone she preferred above all others. All her jewellery was pink, white, or red coral, and gold. It went perfectly with her pale colouring. Her hair was just starting to show silver threads in its Venetian blonde but it looked lovely. Her eyes were deep blue and her nose was straight and long. Her lips were full, and her cheeks were smooth. She wore Persian style robes and, like all the Persian women, wore lots of perfume and make-up. And she shaved her sex. Her eunuchs were by far the best-looking except for Millis, and she tried at least once a day to buy him from me.

She and Sis were not friends. They were not quite enemies, but they were definitely rivals. They were both in love with Alexander.

Alexander was caught right in the middle of two, very strong-willed older women as they vied for his affections. I always suspected Olympias of having carnal relations with her son when he was very young; it would explain his fragility and his violence. Now, however, he seemed to have found a sort of equilibrium and he could face her without the nightmares coming to haunt him.

Sis was the mothering type. She was only happy when she was giving advice, poking her nose into everyone's lives, and generally trying to take over everything. Alexander managed to keep her out of my quarters by promising that I would see her once a day with the children. She was not as harmful as Olympias, but she suffocated Alexander. She was also constantly throwing Stateira at him.

I wondered how he could stand the two women; they were forever barging into his quarters and into his meetings. Once, his patience with them exhausted, he gave orders confining them to the gynaeceum. It was an order that Sis took more or less gracefully, and which made Olympias break every glass object in her rooms.

Sis was more circumspect about what she told the boys. Her stories were all about what they would have to do when ruling Persia and Greece. It did no good when I told her they would never rule; she ignored me. Most of the things they would have to do involved making the sun rise every morning and the springtime come. Not to mention making the flowers grow and the women of the whole kingdom fertile.

'Why do the women need to be fertile?' asked Paul, who sat obediently at her feet munching on the green almonds she peeled for him and popped into his mouth.

'It's time for our swim,' I said, taking Paul's hand and grabbing Chiron before he fell into the chamber pot.

After taking the boys to see Sis and having them stuffed full of honey-cakes and fresh almonds, I spent the rest of the day in my private garden with my sons. There was a swimming pool and I was teaching Chiron to swim. He took to the water like a fish, and soon he was swimming around the whole pool. He was too little to swim on the surface, instead he swam with his head underwater and he'd just poke his little face into the air to breathe. Paul already swam well, and he would follow Chiron around the pool, holding him up when he was tired. I loved seeing their heads, one blond, one light-brown, bent together as they studied an insect walking across the tiles. Chiron thought the sun rose and set on his older brother, and he wanted to do everything he did.

Alexander always managed to come and spent an hour at the pool with us. He loved to swim, and we would float together in the cool, green water. But his respite was short-lived. There were always people to see, petitions to sign, and arguments to resolve. Nothing seemed to be able to function without him.

# Chapter Eleven

At last, things were starting to take shape. Alexander had appointed most of his men to key positions in the government and had begun delegating tasks. He enjoyed spending more time with the visiting diplomats. Setting up trade was one of his strong points. He almost looked happy sitting on his throne surrounded by delegations of foreign merchants.

Kalanos used to sit with Alexander during his discussions with the diplomats. However, one day he sent word he felt too tired to attend, and Usse diagnosed an incurable disease. Kalanos knew there was nothing to be done. He went to Alexander and made one last request. He wished for a funeral pyre, so that he could end his days according to his beliefs. He wanted to be immolated on the day the stars were most auspicious.

I was horrified, but I was the only one who thought it was atrocious. Usse prepared a special potion for Kalanos that would take away pain and Alexander had a huge funeral pyre built according to the old Indian's request.

When the day came for Kalanos to die, he came to see us in my room. He was one of the few to know that Plexis wasn't in fact dead. He put his hand on Plexis's brow and bade him farewell. Then he bowed to me. I bowed back. We didn't touch; he had purified himself before his death and I, as a pregnant woman, was considered impure. I had learned to live with it, though, so it didn't bother me. *Too* much.

'Goodbye, my lady,' he said kindly. 'Think of what I've said and remember only this. Nothing is ever right, or ever wrong. Listen to your heart. I think that is the best advice I can give you.'

'Goodbye, my friend,' I said. My voice was wobbling but I was determined not to cry. He was being so brave, why couldn't I? 'I'll miss you terribly and I'll always remember you. I will try to teach my children all the wise things you were patient enough to teach me.'

Kalanos turned towards Alexander and for the first time his face crumpled. 'O, mighty Sikander,' he said. 'I was blessed to have known you.'

'No, it was I who was blessed.' Alexander swallowed hard, his eyes bright. They embraced. Then Kalanos turned to Usse and took the potion from him. He hugged the doctor, and then hugged Axiom and Brazza. No one cried. We were all stunned.

They left for the funeral ceremony. I, as a woman, couldn't attend of course. I sat down next to Plexis and talked to him. He was a good patient, never grumbling, never complaining. He tried to stay as still as possible, to give his neck a chance to heal, but we worried about him. He had lost a great deal of weight and although Millis took care of him and massaged his muscles, Usse didn't like the way his legs and arms were reacting to so much inaction. They were getting thin and losing muscle tone. Time went by slowly for Plexis. He had been so patient, but in April, after lying perfectly still for six months, his nerves finally frazzled. It started when Usse examined his neck and pronounced him nearly healed.

'Now you can start to move,' he told him.

Plexis smiled then tried to sit up. But even when I helped him he couldn't. His muscles had atrophied and he was too weak. I called Millis and Usse and begged them to do something. Usse suggested Plexis start exercising in the pool, so Millis lifted him up and carried him into the water. There he sat with him in his arms, as Plexis learned to use his legs and arms again.

I sat on the edge of the pool with Chiron on my lap, but the little boy wriggled away and insisted on showing Plexis how well he could dive and swim. I was afraid he'd jostle Plexis and nearly called him back. But when I saw how much Chiron was cheering his father up, I smiled. After a while Plexis became tired so Millis carried him back to his bed. He was no longer flat on his back; he was propped up and could see out the window overlooking our tranquil pool and garden. After that day, he made fast progress, and within a week he was sitting up by himself. His legs were still too weak to hold him, and he had to be carried everywhere, but the pool was helping him greatly. He looked much better. I decided I had to tell him now, before he heard from someone else, or before he asked me for news.

'Plexis?'

The tone of my voice betrayed me, or perhaps his personal antenna picked up my churning emotions. Whatever it was, he put down the scroll he'd been reading and looked at me. 'What is the matter?' he asked.

'I have a confession to make.' I twisted my hands together in my lap and tried to find the right words. 'It's about your wife, about Drypetis. She lost her baby right after we announced your death. I'm sorry.' I said.

He turned his head away and looked out the window. After a while he said, 'Why didn't you tell me sooner?'

'I don't know, I felt guilty. I still do. I was so jealous of her.' My voice dropped to a whisper and I felt my face flaming.

He turned to face me, his eyes wide in surprise.

'Jealous? You? Of Drypetis? But, but …' He winced when he tried to sit up. 'I keep forgetting I can't move yet. Ashley, just tell me what happened. What happened to Drypetis? Why do you feel guilty?'

'When you had your accident, I told Usse to bring you to my room.' I said, not meeting his gaze. 'And I said that no one could come to see you. I did send a message to your wife, telling her she could come. It said, "Come right away, your husband needs you." But she wrote back, saying that she'd rather die than set foot in my quarters, and she ordered me to bring you to her rooms. She said that she would allow Usse to treat you, and that she would do everything I asked, but that you had to stay with her. She even offered to empty her quarters, so that you would be alone with just her, Usse, and Alexander … and that I would be able to visit whenever I wished.'

'And you refused.' His voice was curiously flat.

'I had to.'

'You didn't trust her.' He turned his face towards the

window again.

'I didn't at the time. I don't know now. Should I have trusted her? I think sometimes that if I'd let you go to her, she would have said nothing. Perhaps she would have gone ahead with the plan, and she would have pretended to mourn your death. She could have stayed with us, lived with us, and maybe she wouldn't have lost your baby.'

Plexis was silent a long time. Then he turned towards me. 'I don't know what she would have done. She hated you. She wouldn't let me touch her for the entire time I was in Ecbatana. It was as if I had to do penance for having dared make love to you. She thought you deserved to die. I don't think she would have been able to keep the secret. I'm sorry about the child. In the back of my mind he was always there, a baby in Ecbatana. Now you say *he* died when *I* was supposed to. Are the gods mocking us, do you suppose?'

'I don't know. I'm sorry, Plexis. If you're angry with me, I understand.'

He looked at me, his expression inscrutable, then turned back to the window. 'Angry? No, I am not. You love me, and you were jealous. I can understand that. You were trying to protect me, and an innocent girl lost her child because of it. I feel sorrow, that is all.'

I put folded my hands on my round stomach and bowed my head. 'There is still time,' I said. 'If you still love her I will send for her. We will figure out a way to tell her you're still alive. When you have recovered, you and Drypetis can go anywhere in the world together.'

He gave a sigh. 'No, Ashley. Where could Drypetis go

and still be happy? She could only be happy in her own world. She was raised to be a Persian princess. She has never set foot upon a floor that was not part of a palace. She has always travelled in a curtained litter, and she never once thought of parting the curtains to look outside at the world. She never went out of the palace to see what was beyond its walls. She lives in her tiny bejewelled world, and she is incapable of leaving it. If I took her away from her surroundings, she would be frightened and horrified. She could never love me if I weren't somebody important. She is a princess.'

'Do you still love her?'

'Sometimes I still think of her, I won't lie to you.' He turned away from me.

We were silent for a while. Plexis had made his voice kind, but I'd heard a spark of … something … in it. I couldn't tell what he was thinking. Was he angry or sorrowful? Finally I touched his hand and he turned to face me. He'd been crying silently. Tears left faint traces on his pale cheeks but his eyes were clear. I felt terrible. I realized that my selfishness had robbed him of a chance to see his wife again.

'I'm sorry,' I said. 'I wish I had done everything differently. I should have spoken to you before making any decisions. I wish I could do it over again, but I don't regret saving your life.' I stopped and shook my head. 'I'll never regret saving you. I only feel badly about Drypetis. If only I had another chance!'

'What would you have done?' He was curious.

'I would have told you sooner. Because of my petty

jealousy, you lost a wife and a child. It's my fault.'

'Your fault, or the gods' fault, it matters not,' said Plexis. 'What is done is done, I will not look back. I think you should learn to do the same.' A tiny flash of humour shone briefly in his eyes. 'You spend far too much time fretting about time.'

I was startled, but he would always surprise me. As soon as I thought I'd figured him out, he'd change. Plexis was more complicated than Alexander in some ways.

It was now the month of May. A beautiful spring month. I was blooming with the flowers. Alexander cupped his hands around my huge belly and laughed delightedly each time he felt the baby kick.

'I said you'd be huge,' he said, grinning happily.

'I'm much bigger than with my other children,' I said, shaking my head. 'Usse says it's normal, each pregnancy makes you bigger.'

'For your next one you'll look like an elephant.' Alexander tipped his head to one side, probably imagining me as an elephant. From him, that was a compliment.

He was in high spirits this morning because that afternoon he was going on a hunt with two guests, ambassadors from the faraway countries of Gaul and Iberia. I knew the places as France and Spain, but I supposed they were different from when I'd last seen them. We welcomed ambassadors from Carthage, Gaul, Eire, Britain, Ethiopia, and a man even came all the way from the wilderness of the Black Forest to see Iskander the Great Conqueror.

These ambassadors were completely unlike the men in business suits who would roam the embassies of the future. Neither of them had ever seen a barber. The Gaul's hair hung past his shoulders in matted locks, and the Iberian had used clay to form huge spikes in his hair. The Gaul wore a long grey robe and carried a staff, and the Iberian wore a woollen blanket that smelled like a goat. Both men were awed by Alexander's court. The court was not as awed by them. At that time, the Persians were refined and wore brightly coloured robes and fancy hats. The Greeks didn't wear many clothes, but they were finicky about cleanliness and shaving.

I wondered if I wanted to venture north to Gaul. After all, without the Eiffel Tower, the Louvre, and the Champs-Élysées, what was left of France? And if everyone were as malodorous as these two men, the whole country must simply reek.

They had come bearing gifts. The man from Gaul had brought offerings of salt pork and cheese. Alexander had received them with without blinking. The dried, salted pork haunch was carried to the kitchen where the cooks looked at it from every angle before hanging it up as a decoration. The cheese was carefully removed from the palace by a brave slave and taken as far into the marshes as possible.

The Iberian had brought three pitch-black bulls, which were very useful. Black animals were sacrificed to the god of the dead, Hades. My ex-husband, as most people assumed. They called him Pluto, the 'rich one', because underground is where the gold, silver, and jewels are found. The Greeks, I discovered, panicked completely at the idea of going underground. They were afraid of stumbling into the underworld by mistake.

Alexander was most interested in the Gaul's description of their houses. According to the Gaul they had glass-paned windows, something even the Greeks hadn't thought of.

I smiled at my husband. The years hadn't dimmed his enthusiasm for anything new, and his passion for discovery was still the driving force behind him. He wanted to learn everything, to understand everything, and use that knowledge to make his world a better place. I sighed. He turned to me, a comical expression on his face.

'Why do you look at me like that?' he asked.

'How?'

'With your heart in your eyes. I told you to be careful, the gods are jealous.'

'I can't help it,' I admitted. 'I'm still madly in love with you, Iskander of Macedonia. The years go by, and still I find my eyes drawn to you and my heart follows.'

He smiled blindingly. His face softened. But before he could reply, a small cough was heard. We both turned to find Nassar, our faithful translator, standing in front of us.

'My lady. Iskander, my lord, I have come to inform you that another ambassador has come to see you. From the kingdom of Rome.'

'Yes?' Alexander said, raising his eyebrows.

'Well, it seems that the Gaul and the Roman are fighting, I just thought maybe you'd like to come and try to separate them.'

'Fighting?' I asked, getting to my feet rather clumsily.

'Well, I'm not sure how it started, my lady, but I think the Roman said something nasty about the Gaul's cheese and it went downhill from there.'

# Chapter Twelve

One thing I hated about Babylon: there were millions of mosquitoes. I made sure that we rubbed citronella over ourselves, and I burned dried herbs in our rooms to keep them away. At night, we slept within tents of fine muslin and that certainly helped. Unfortunately, during the hot days there was not much we could do.

At last, the funeral pyre for Plexis was lit and the funeral games could begin. Over three thousand men took part in the sports. I didn't see any of it. Women were not invited to see or participate in the games. I stayed in my quarters with Plexis, whose funeral it was. Smoke from the burning pyre made our eyes sting and throats ache for days. We were glad when the funeral was over, except that the pall of smoke had kept the mosquitoes at bay.

The city was built near a great swamp. It was a wonderful place, full of wild animals and thousands of different kinds of wildfowl and birds. Alexander often went there to hunt. Hunting was one of his favourite sports, and now that he had elephants, it was even more fantastic. The great beasts would wade into the swamp, and from their broad backs, Alexander would shoot duck and deer with his bow and arrows. He was an excellent shot and often brought back venison and duck for our dinners. I was worried about poison so it was the only meat the children would eat.

Also that month, Alexander gave me Chirpa. There was a terrible row with Stateira about that, but I wouldn't back down. Thankfully, Alexander didn't either. I freed Chirpa, and she asked to stay with me. I told her about Plexis. I trusted her completely. In return, she made sure he was never bored or lonely. Soon I was used to seeing her bright head bowed over his dark one as they spoke softly together in the cool gloom of my bedroom.

A strange thing happened that month, although I didn't see it. Each evening Alexander set aside an hour for sports. It was one of the only times the different tribes got along. Alexander was a fervent believer in games. The Olympic Games was a sports festival set aside for men. Another, in honour of Zeus's queen, Hera, was for women and took place every four years.

Alexander's soldiers were always ready for games, so there wasn't a day that something wasn't organized. Each tribe excelled in a different sport, so some days there would be foot races, some days wrestling, or polo, or archery. The men would meet in the great plain on the north side of the city, and they would compete in front of a large crowd of delighted spectators. Afterwards, just before sunset, they would make their way back to the palace and wash and get ready for dinner. Usually there was a great deal of laughing and teasing between the winners and losers.

That day, while everyone was at the sports field, a man climbed over the garden wall, donned the royal cloak and the royal crown of Persia, and sat on Alexander's chair. He sat there until everyone came back into the garden. Alexander's men had been talking loudly and jostling each other, when suddenly they caught sight of the strange figure. Silence descended upon them. Unfortunately, the first men in the garden were Persians. To them, the king was divine. The crown of Persia was a holy relic and to touch it was a sacrilege. No one knew what to do. When they warily approached the man, he smiled and nodded at them exactly as if he were the king. It gave them the chills.

Then Alexander arrived, hot, sweaty, and in a terrible mood because his polo team had lost and he hated losing. He saw the man on his throne and he frowned. 'Who are you, and what are you doing here?' he asked.

The man stared back with wide, innocent eyes, and Alexander realized that he was a simpleton, a man with the mind of a child. 'The gods told me that the throne would soon be empty. They said that the crown would soon seek a head, and that the cape would cover a coffin.' He smiled brightly. 'They told me to come here and take the king's place.'

The Persian guards were shocked beyond words. Silently they raised their spears, ready to kill him there and then.

Alexander was shocked as well, but he couldn't help comparing the man on the throne with his idiot brother, Arrhidaeus, the one his mother had poisoned as a babe, making him retarded. The guilt he'd always felt towards his brother was tremendous. Alexander swallowed hard, trying not to vomit. His brother was older than he was. By rights, Arrhidaeus should have inherited his father's throne, not him. Now an idiot was sitting on his throne. All at once the sun was too bright, and his head felt as if it would split open. 'Take him away, find out where his family is and give him back to them. Tell them to take better care of him, or next time he will be killed,' said Alexander to the men. The Persians were furious; they'd wanted to sacrifice the man that evening. The Greeks and Egyptians thought it was an evil omen, and the Macedonians mostly thought it was wildly funny. Alexander didn't think it was funny. He went to bathe, and didn't speak of the incident for a very long time.

Part of the problem lay in the fact that he'd left the crown and cloak where someone could take them. It was like leaving the true cross and grail lying around to a Catholic, for example, or accidentally backing your bulldozer into the Wailing Wall if you were a Jew. To the Persians it was terrible sacrilege. They were horrified at the whole thing and Alexander's reputation suffered greatly in the eyes of his Persian guards.

I think Alexander realized this, and he felt guilty about that too. He wasn't particularly religious, and he certainly didn't take himself for a god. However, I believe that he felt very keenly the disappointment of his Persian subjects. Since he had always been determined to be respectful to everyone's religion, he redoubled his efforts. He took part in all the religious ceremonies that month, even the Persian ones that he would sometimes skip before, trying to make up for his former lack of respect.

# Chapter Thirteen

In the month of May, the weather took a turn for the worse. Thunderstorms boomed over the city and there were swarms of hungry mosquitoes at night. Alexander had to oversee religious celebrations, some lasting until very late, and one evening he came back with a slight chill. I didn't think much of it. Usse gave him some hot tea, and we lay down in bed. Plexis was already asleep, lying in his own bed next to ours. The mosquito netting moved slightly in the breeze. It was much cooler than it had been all week; the rain had cleared the air. During the night, Alexander developed a high fever. The next morning he could hardly move, his muscles cramped and he was drenched in sweat. It was malaria.

'How do you feel now?' I asked him for the hundredth time that day, after Usse gave him his medicine.

Alexander opened one eye and stared at me. It was his blue eye, I noticed. 'I would feel better if my head stopped hurting,' he admitted. 'The fever is making me thirsty. Do you have any water nearby?'

'Of course.'

I poured water from the pitcher into his golden cup and held it for him as he drank. The muscles in his throat worked as the water went down. Then he lay back on the bed with a sigh. 'Do I die of malaria then?' he asked. He tried to grin, but his mouth trembled suddenly. I leaned down and kissed him on his lips. They were hot and dry despite the cool drink.

'Are you afraid?'

'I thought I wouldn't be.' He took a shaky breath and let it out slowly. 'But that was when I thought the only thing that counted was my kingdom.'

'And now?' I asked him.

'I've had time to think. When you saved Plexis that's when things began to change for me. I realized something I hadn't known before. I want to stay with you. I love you, Ashley of the Sacred Sandals. I have told you that twice before. I should have said it more. Now, with this fever making my bones ache, I will tell you a third time. I want to see the babe you carry. I want to grow old surrounded by my loved ones. I no longer want to die. Does that answer your question? Yes, I am afraid.'

'Don't be afraid. I love you too, Alex.'

'So why do you cry?' He reached a hand to my cheek and brushed tears away.

'Because I never dared hope that you would let go of your dream.' My tears fell faster now. Teardrops sparkled on his hands like diamonds.

'It took me long enough to understand that my dream was an empty one without you and Plexis by my side, and that my future was an illusion. Ashley, don't cry. Please. I feel as if I've woken up from a long nightmare. All the battles and bloodshed, all the good men who died following me, they will lie on my conscious for ever. Only you will be able to ease my mind. You have seen the future, so you can tell me that it was not all futile.'

'Of course not, Alexander. Nothing you did was futile.'

'It feels that way now,' he said. His eyes were very bright. I frowned at him. He was starting to sound distinctly un-Alexander-like. I put my hand on his forehead and jerked it back with a muffled cry. He was burning up.

'Usse! Usse!' I cried.

Usse came running and started dosing him with quinine. Alexander's symptoms eased enough to allow him to go to the various meetings he had with his generals, and for him to make the sacrifices required of him as king – and god – of Persia.

I fretted and paced in my rooms, Chiron tagging after me, tugging on my skirt, asking me to play with him. To take my mind off Alexander's sickness I sat on the edge of the pool and watched as Chiron showed me his new accomplishment, a real, head-first dive into the water.

I took my sons to see my mother-in-law Olympias, who had heard of Alexander's illness, and who gave me one of her sacred snakes.

'Put it around his neck and let him sleep with it,' she said, her beautiful eyes serious. 'The snake has been blessed and will absorb all the poison in his body.'

'He hasn't been poisoned,' I said, startled.

Olympias smiled. 'All Alexander's illnesses are caused by poison. A god cannot get sick, so he must have been poisoned.'

I took the grass snake coiled up in a woven basket just big enough to hold it. It was harmless, and I wasn't afraid, but I wasn't about to share my bed with a snake. 'Thank you,' I said, bowing. I was learning diplomacy.

Then I had to go see Sis, and she gave me remedies for Alexander's illness. Hers were a handful of amulets, a parchment with a spell written on it, and a jar full of something noxious that smelled as if it had died years ago. I thanked her, called to Chiron and Paul who were playing a board game with one of her slaves, and we went back to my rooms. The day passed slowly. It rained again and steam rose from the hot tiles around the pool.

Alexander came back that evening and was well enough to bathe alone and dine but that night he was ill again. The fever came back and he became delirious. He always had a high temperature, but now it seemed to soar. Usse gave him more quinine and willow-bark tea. He slept, but fitfully. It was May 31$^{st}$.

Eumenes, the faithful secretary, took down Usse's words every morning on how Alexander spent his nights. He wrote things like this:

"June 1$^{st}$: The King made the necessary sacrifices in the temple and then retired to his quarters. After bathing, he went to his chamber and played dice, then he slept but during the night had an excess of fever. He spent an agitated night.

June 3$^{rd}$: After another bath he went to the temple to make the ritual sacrifices. He spoke to Nearchus about the next expedition, and then retired to his rooms where he dined. That evening the fever returned and he spent the night in the bathroom." (*This was true. His fever was so high that Usse laid him on the cool tiles in the bathroom to try to ease his pain. Alexander's skin became so sensitive that we could hardly touch him without him crying out.*)

"June 4th: The day was spent at the poolside. The fever was very strong and wouldn't go down. His officers came to see him and they discussed filling vacant posts in the army. He told them to appoint men with experience.

June 6th: The fever still raged. He was carried in a litter to the temple where he assisted in the rituals, and then he went back to his rooms where he slept poorly.

June 7th: The fever still wouldn't leave him. He was transported to the Grand Palace to meet with his generals but he could barely speak to them and it seemed as if he was delirious." – Plutarch, *Alexander the Great.*

By now, Usse and I were concerned. Alexander seemed to have caught a particularly virulent form of malaria, certainly from one of his hunts in the swamps. It seemed that the quinine and the willow-bark tea weren't helping him. He hardly slept, but spent all day and night tossing and turning. His muscles hurt, his abdomen was sore, and his fever gave him appalling headaches. His eyes were glazed and he hardly knew where he was.

On the 8th of June Eumenes wrote: "All day long he had an enormous fever as well as that night." – Plutarch, *Alexander the Great.*

Usse came to me that afternoon. 'My lady, if the fever continues he will not live two more days. His life is in grave danger. What shall we do now?'

I had been expecting this. I had one last chance to save him. It all depended on his sickness. Malaria, if I remembered correctly, was caused not by infection or a virus, but by a parasite in the bloodstream. Fever didn't kill it, but cold could. Of course, there were no refrigerators here, no freezers to make ice, and the nearest snow was on the mountain top, a year's march away.

'Ashley?' It was Plexis. He had been watching Alexander's decline with barely concealed panic. The inability to move was driving him mad. Even Usse couldn't calm his fears.

'What is it?' It was nearly dawn. I'd spent a sleepless night at Alexander's bedside. I wanted Usse to get some rest, and I managed to convince him to leave me alone with my husband. Usse had already gone without sleep for three nights, and I would need him later. I brushed a lock of hair out of my eyes and leaned over Plexis, a smile on my lips.

'Don't look at me like that,' he said.

'Like what?' I was surprised.

'Like I'm a cranky child. I've been trying so hard to be good.' His voice broke. 'I lie here and I hear everything that's going on, but I can't get up to see you, or Iskander. I am frightened. I fear that he will die, and that nothing you or Usse can do will save him. I know that neither you nor Iskander could sleep last night. I heard how ill he was. Tell me, Ashley, will he live?'

'There is nothing Usse or I can do,' I said sadly.

'Nothing?' His hands clenched the sides of his bed and I saw the pulse in his throat beat faster.

'There *is* something that might save him,' I said slowly. 'But, Plexis, I'll not lie to you. Iskander is gravely ill.'

'That I know,' he said. His voice wavered. 'What shall

we do?'

'We pray,' I said. 'That's all we can do right now.'

'If you wanted to make me feel better you've just failed miserably,' he said.

I took a sharp breath and looked out the window where the dawn tinted the sky deep gold. 'I wish I could do something more, but I can't.' My voice was little more than a whisper.

I was lying. I knew something nobody in that world could ever suspect. I knew that a time-travelling journalist was on his way to interview Alexander on his deathbed.

Thirty years before I was born, a journalist had come to interview Alexander the Great. The transcripts from the interview were disappointing, to say the least. The Institute of Time Travel had put a red flag on that file. It was marked as a failure, but no reason was given. The Institute kept its secrets. According to the report I was able to access, Alexander had been in a coma, delirious with fever, and unable to answer any questions. It was part of the mystery that made me want to interview the young king when he was twenty-three years old.

I'd been with him for almost ten years now. For all that time I'd kept this a secret. And I'd waited. Now it was time.

We moved Alexander to the Grand Palace and I spent my time going back and forth from my room to his. One thing that seems to be true about late pregnancy: I didn't need much sleep. I grabbed quick naps now and then, but otherwise I was wide awake and full of a nervous energy that made my hands tingle.

That night I spoke to Usse. He already knew a great deal, but now I told him about my coming from the future. The doctor took it more or less in his stride. It didn't change his attitude about me. However, I needed to tell him everything. I would have to tell him, because I needed his help. I couldn't carry Alexander by myself, and we had to act quickly.

As usual, he listened to me silently. His thoughts remained hidden behind his inscrutable gaze. When I finished, he reached over and took my hands in his. 'Thank you for telling me all this,' he said. 'I will do as you ask of me.'

'Do you think I'm wrong to try to save him?' I asked.

'Only the future will tell,' said Usse.

'No, I want to hear your opinion,' I said. 'You have no idea how guilty I feel.'

'Do you feel badly about Plexis?'

'Yes, in a way I do.'

'You saved him from death.'

'But don't you see? In a way, he *is* dead! When he recovers, the only thing he can do is leave. He can never see any of his friends or family again. Because of me, he lost his wife, and she lost her baby. I have no idea where he'll go, or if he'll want to stay with us.'

'He doesn't blame you for any of that,' said Usse, his voice soft. 'I've spoken to him often.'

'Perhaps not, but I blame myself. It's the same for Iskander. It will be as if he's dead, and I'm starting to wonder if I truly have the right to do this.'

'He would do the same for you, if he could,' said Usse.

I sighed deeply and nodded. 'I love him so much that I would sacrifice his kingdom. I only hope that someday he'll forgive me.'

'But, Ashley, don't you understand? You are changing nothing. If what you tell me is the truth, if you do nothing he will die. If we save him, he must seem to be dead to the world. I do believe you Ashley. I believe your story. Therefore I know I must help you. I feel as if I have been chosen for something important. I will not fail you, and you will not fail Iskander.'

I hoped that he was right. I also hoped it wasn't too late, because then this whole conversation would have been for nothing.

The next day was the worst. Alexander was in a coma and all his generals and companions lined up outside the palace demanding to see him. News of his illness had become so grave that they thought he was already dead.

Eumenes, Alexander's secretary, wrote this; "The soldiers and generals were taken with a violent desire to see Iskander. For some, because they longed to see him while he was still alive; for others because rumour had it he was already dead and the royal guard was keeping it a secret. But most, feeling most keenly pain and love for their young king, came to see Iskander. As the army filed in front of his bed, he was already past speaking. However this didn't keep him from greeting each and every man by raising his head with a great effort, and acknowledging them with his expressive eyes." – Arrien, *Anabase d'Alexandre VII, 25, 1-26, 3.*

We let them come in. One by one, they filed by Alexander's bed. He tried to speak to them. It broke my heart to see him. He clasped each man by the hand, and his great eyes spoke volumes, even if his throat could not. The men were deeply shocked at his appearance. His colour was bad, his breathing hoarse, and his hand, when they took it, was burning hot. More than one man cried out in surprise and horror. All of them were crying when they left the room.

That same evening Seleucos and Ptolemy Lagos went to the oracle and begged it to tell them what to do. The oracle was remarkably clear and concise that night. 'Do nothing,' it said. 'Leave him alone. And whatever you do, don't move him.'

I had paid a great amount of gold to have the sibyl say that.

The next morning was June 9th. Alexander was in a coma.

I kissed him tenderly on the mouth. He didn't move. He was wasting away from the fever; in a few hours, he would be dead.

I sat at the foot of his bed, waiting for the man who would come from three thousand years in the future. He would come that afternoon. Meanwhile, I had Usse and Millis prepared for action.

Millis was to follow the man and tell us where he went after he left Alexander's bedside. Usse and I would carry Alexander to where the time-traveller would find the tractor beam for his return.

Time-travel is a stomach-wrenching experience that

takes your atoms apart, freezes them, and then puts them back together after submitting them to a magnetic beam fixed on the year of choice. There is a complicated explanation involving relativity, time warps, and various factors such as speed of light and folding space. I never learned the mechanics of it. I did know that the magnetic beam froze you.

Alexander's only chance to survive lay in that freezing cold magnetic beam.

The time-traveller came right on time.

At noon, the last of the tearful generals and companions left. They were destroyed. None of them could utter a coherent word after seeing their king lying so ill on his bed.

An hour passed. The sun beat on the roof and the temperature climbed into the hundreds. A deaf slave waved a fan over Alexander, stirring the air like hot soup. Usse and I watched silently as he lay dying.

Then a man walked into the throne-room. He was uncertain, walking slowly, and I was wryly amused to see that he limped from his shabby grass sandals. He wore an unbleached linen loincloth and I knew that a tradi-scope implanted in his head would translate everything that we said to him, and that the amulet hanging from a chain around his neck was a recorder.

He hesitated as he approached. No one had accompanied him. I'd given orders to let him come in alone. When he was ten feet away he stopped and prostrated himself, touching his forehead to the ground. He'd studied the Persian protocol before coming. Usse motioned him to approach, and I stood up and greeted him. He saw that I was pregnant. It was obvious I was going to give birth any day.

Roxanne was pregnant too. She had been terrified that Alexander would kill her, so she had tried to hide it for as long as possible. Alexander had gone to see her just a month ago. He told her not to worry, that her children would always be welcome. She was thankful but deeply suspicious. Now she wouldn't let anyone but her own slaves near her, keeping to the gynaeceum.

Lysimachus, the father of her child, stayed away from us as well. Alexander had never said anything to him, but Roxanne was busy plotting to claim the crown after Alexander's death. She wanted to make Lysimachus king. She had come to see Alexander once since he was ill. She'd sidled into the throne room, her eyes darting, her face pale. I had to clench my fists to keep from slapping her when she asked Usse, in a high, childlike voice, when Alexander would die. Usse lowered his own murderous gaze at her and told her that his life was in the hands of the gods and that she should go back to her rooms and pray.

She had gone back to her rooms, but not to pray. Instead, she'd sent for Lysimachus and together they started to scheme.

I knew all this from Nassar, my ever-faithful translator. He was working in the palace with the diplomatic corps. He was not one of the people I'd trusted with my secret; he was a good spy, but an awful gossip. He told everything about Roxanne and Lysimachus, and my history lessons had told me the rest.

Roxanne would perish in the civil war between Olympias and Cassander, a pawn because of her ambitions. Her son would die too, and Lysimachus, who would ultimately triumph, would declare war against Seleucos in Persia and would get killed by his former companion-in-arms.

All this was upsetting to me, especially when I saw my two former friends nearly every day. Lysimachus was becoming increasingly distant, and Seleucos, already satrap of Persia, would soon become absolute ruler and founder of a dynasty. At least, under his rule, Persia would bloom and know centuries of glory.

Olympias had come to see Alexander every day since he fell ill. Already she was hysterical with grief. I hoped that she would stay away until that evening. Her wailing got on my nerves. Sis was even worse. She dressed in black and walked around the entire palace, her face covered in ashes. Of course, when Olympias saw that, she had to rub ashes over *her* face, and soon the two queens were having a mourning contest, although Alexander wasn't even dead.

As I expected, the time-traveller asked Alexander several questions and was bitterly disappointed to see that he was incapable of speech. He turned to Usse and asked if he thought Alexander would be able to speak to him.

'It will be as the gods wish,' said Usse in a solemn voice.

The time-traveller looked at me nervously. He wasn't sure if he could speak to me directly or not. Finally, he asked me, 'Are you Roxanne?'

I choked, but decided it was best to pretend to be Roxanne. 'Yes.'

'You're expecting a child?'

'I am.'

He was flustered by my short answers, but because Alexander was unconscious, I was the next best person to interview. I could sense his journalist's mind ticking. 'So, your husband just got back from India?' he asked.

I shrugged. 'Yes.'

There's something aggravating about 'yes' and 'no' answers. Journalists hate them. He tried to draw me out. 'What did he think about it?'

'He loved India,' I said bleakly.

'Ah. And he fought Porus and Musicanus.' He'd done his homework better than I. 'What about Hephaestion?'

'What about him?' I asked cautiously.

'Did his death cause your husband much pain?'

I darted a glance at Usse who was frowning at the man. 'Of course,' I said. 'They were best friends. Wouldn't you be upset if your best friend died?'

'What about the stories I hear about him being a god? Is he really the son of Zeus?'

'The Persians think he's the son of Zeus-Amon,' I said. 'But the Greeks and the Macedonians do not. I, coming from Bactria, do not.'

'I see. What did he like best about India?'

'The elephants.'

'Oh.' That wasn't what he wanted to hear. 'And did he give any indications about what would happen, uh, in case he died?' He was walking on thin ice now and he knew it.

'No.' I decided to go back to my monosyllables. I looked over at Alexander and my heart gave a lurch. His face was waxen. I could see his chest rising and falling with the effort of his breathing, and the heat of his fever seemed to radiate off his body. I touched his face gently and tears welled up in my eyes.

The man drew a deep breath and addressed Usse again. He was a good journalist; he didn't give up easily. 'Did you follow him on his travels?' he asked.

Usse smiled sadly and nodded. 'I went to the ends of the earth and back with him,' he said.

'Why? Why go so far?'

'Because I love him.'

The answer was simple but seemed to stymie the journalist. He glanced at me again and asked, 'And you, my lady Roxanne, did you see any of his battles?'

I closed my eyes and tears leaked from beneath my lids. 'I saw only one, the one he fought against Porus. It was a horrible fight. Ten thousand good men died.'

'You saw that battle?' His voice held a note of interest now. 'And tell me, was it true he built twelve altars to the gods near the river Beas?'

'It's true, he did have them built,' I said wearily. I wished he'd stop talking about things I didn't want to think about . 'He built them on a small rise overlooking the river. They were ... they are beautiful. An artist carved my face on one.' My voice tapered off. I shook my head, and looked bleakly at Alexander. For a heart-stopping minute I thought he'd died, but then I caught sight of a fluttering breath and my shoulders sagged in relief. He was still with us.

The man only had a limited time here then he had to return to his appointment with the magnetic beam or be forced to live in 323 BC. He had no intention of staying. He kept glancing at his wrist where, of course, there was no watch. Then he looked out the window where the shadows were growing long.

A guard came in, leading one of the envoys and a translator. I recognized the man from Gaul. He wanted to pay his respects, he told me, speaking through the translator.

I nodded, and glanced at the journalist, who was leaning forward expectantly.

The Gaul put down his staff, knelt, and touched his head to the floor. Then he stood and began to chant. While chanting, he bent over and pressed one hand to his chest, and the other on Alexander's forehead. I half rose, meaning to stop him, but the Gaul stepped back, picked up the staff he'd placed near the bed, and left, his translator and the guard at his heels. Usse and I looked at each other. What had *that* been about?

The journalist, too, looked disappointed. Perhaps he'd thought the Gaul could miraculously heal Alexander. Poor fellow. His interview had been a disaster.

Olympias came and did her wailing and hair-tearing act. Then Sis entered the throne room, and together, the two queens made quite a show. The journalist watched everything with wide eyes. Sis had shaved her head, and her face and hands were gray with ashes. Olympias hadn't cut her lovely hair *too* short, she was far too vain, but she was covered with soot. Both were dressed in black robes, trailing ashes in their wakes. When I remember the palace of Nebuchadnezzar, that is the image I see—black robes and ashes.

When the queens had wailed and gnashed their teeth enough, Usse stepped forward and quietly yet firmly asked both women to leave. They walked away, sobbing loudly. Each queen trying to sob louder than the other.

After the queens left there were a few moments of blessed silence as the sun sank below the horizon and the sky darkened. Cool air stole into the room, and I sent the deaf slave away. The slave bowed to me, and to Alexander, then left on silent feet, carrying his fan on his shoulders. I looked out the window and watched as clouds moved across the sky, hiding the first pale stars. There was a taste of ashes in my mouth.

A few more questions about India, and the journalist rose to his feet and took his leave. He looked dejected. I could sympathize with him. He had travelled all the way back to Alexander's time to stare at a man in a coma and watch two mad women screaming while a very pregnant woman sat and cried. His report was going to be a dismal failure.

Millis stepped out from behind the curtain where he'd been hiding. In the dusk, the whites of his eyes shone. He was frightened.

At a discrete signal from Usse, Millis followed the journalist. Usse and I took Alexander's litter and trailed them at a distance.

I was big-bellied and clumsy, but my pregnancies never

made me weak. I carried the litter easily. Alexander had wasted away during his illness, and I was shocked at how little he weighed. I hoped that my plan would work. Otherwise, we could do nothing to save him. He would die that night.

Millis came back to get us and motioned for us to hurry. The magnetic beam had deposited the man in an empty alleyway not far from the palace's garbage dump. An out-of-the-way place with no prying eyes.

I saw the tell-tale blue light beginning to form in a dark corner and said to Usse, 'We must hold him inside until he is frozen, then we will have to fight to wrench him out again.'

'Very well, my lady,' said Usse. His eyes were wide, and a nerve in his cheek began to twitch.

Millis looked terrified, but he swallowed bravely and took Alexander under the arms, lifting him off the stretcher. He and Usse would have to do everything; I couldn't help. Already I felt ominous cramps in my lower back. The baby kicked.

The time-traveller stepped into the sparkling beam. He had his back to us and didn't see us coming. When Alexander was thrust inside the beam with him, he panicked. He tried to shove him out, but Millis and Usse held fast.

Alexander turned silver. Millis stared in horror as his own arms suddenly became covered with pale, glittery frost. Usse had been warned; he set his jaw and held onto Alexander.

The time-traveller tried one last time to push Alexander

from the beam. He opened his mouth several times but was incapable of speech. He was almost frozen. Then there was a massive jolt as the beam tried to accommodate the two men. Usse and Millis used all their strength to hold Alexander firmly within the light. I watched helplessly as the time-traveller was ejected from the beam. He flew against the courtyard and hit the wall with a sickening crunch. He had been frozen and the shock killed him. He was dead before he hit the ground. I put my hands to my mouth. I was overcome by nausea.

The man was dead. Suddenly I remembered what the oracle had told me: that I would kill a man in order to return to my own time. I looked at the beam and gave a sharp cry. If I wanted to, I could go back to my own time. I had to decide immediately because in a few moments it would be too late. I reached towards the shimmering blue column; the urge to escape was instinctive and strong. I felt the need to flee, to rush into the beam and return to my place and time. The urge lasted only a second. Then I drew a deep breath. I would never abandon my husband or my children. If Alexander died, it was too late for regrets. I'd lived ten years with the man I loved. Tears pricked my eyes. I would never regret loving him, and I wouldn't run away now.

Alexander began to freeze. I watched as frost bloomed on his arms and legs, as his face silvered and his hair turned sparkling white. His breathing slowed and stopped. His eyes glazed over as a film of ice formed on them. Soon a scintillating coat of frozen water covered him. His body turned lavender and shimmered. Then he started to vanish.

'Now!' I screamed. Millis and Usse pulled backwards. There was a huge tug-of-war; the beam was incredibly strong and it didn't want to give up the body within it.

But just as Alexander had torn me from its grasp more than ten years ago, so Usse and Millis yanked Alexander out in a shower of flashing blue and silver sparks. There was a sound like a chorus of moans, and the beam disappeared. We placed Alexander carefully on the stretcher. Now we had to carry him to my room and we had to wait. Before we left, I turned to the time-travelling journalist, lying dead near the wall. I searched for his amulet recorder, but it was nowhere to be found. It must have fallen off in the scuffle and had been sent back to the future.

He had been a middle-aged man, maybe forty or so. He didn't look like Alexander, but he would have to do. I told Millis to take him and to place his body on Alexander's bed in the Grand Palace, cut his hair, like Alexander's, and cover him with a linen sheet. The journalist didn't have any of Alexander's scars, but he did have warm brown hair. He was dead, and in death, would impersonate Alexander.

I hoped that Alexander would live.

In the heat of the sultry night, the ice was already starting to melt off Alexander's face and hair. Rivulets of water ran down his neck and chest. His body was still blue and sheathed in ice. He was frozen. He looked dead. He wasn't even breathing. I was afraid to feel for a heartbeat.

We carried Alexander to my room and put him, stretcher and all, on the bed. I sat on a chair, but I couldn't rest. We didn't have a minute to spare. I looked at Usse and he gazed back at me.

'Did you tell Nearchus we were coming?' I whispered.

'I did. The boat is waiting. We'll leave as soon as it's fully dark.'

'What did he say when you told him Plexis was still alive?' I asked.

'He said, "By Hades and Persephone!" and then he blanched. He knew it was you. He said he would do anything you asked if you could save Iskander.'

'Thank you, Usse. I don't know if I can ever repay you, but I promise I'll try.'

'I know that, but I've been repaid. I have been chosen to save my king.' His handsome face brightened as he smiled, but his dark eyes were still worried.

Suddenly we heard a sound. A piece of ice fell on the floor. Usse and I leapt to Alexander's side. I grabbed Usse's arm to stay upright. 'He's alive,' I gasped. Shock and relief made my nose bleed, and I started to laugh. I felt unhinged, but Usse sank to his knees next to Alexander's bed.

'Can you hear us?' he asked.

Alexander opened his eyes briefly. His teeth started to chatter and his skin lost its bluish tint. Slowly his cheeks turned pink, then his nose. He tried to speak but couldn't. Usse bent over him, wiping the melting ice crystals off his neck and chest. Alexander seemed to know us, and I thought he tried to smile. Then he started to shiver violently.

Usse gave him a drink of willow-bark tea and he sipped

it, the first thing he had been able to drink in two days. Afterwards Alexander closed his eyes and passed out.

Millis had already carried Plexis to the boat. I shuddered to think what would have happened if anyone caught them. Luckily, everything was chaos that night.

I woke my sleeping boys, and Chirpa helped me get their baggage. We were leaving Babylon like thieves in the night, carrying with us only the barest necessities. The city was plunged into a supernatural darkness. No one had lit the street lamps. Windows were dark. Thunder growled, and sheet lightning flickered through the sky illuminating the huge ziggurat. From the palace came an eerie wailing. My hair stood on end.

When I climbed into the boat, I put the boys into their hammocks and I smoothed Paul's bright hair off his forehead.

'Where's Father?' he asked.

I smiled tenderly at my son. 'He'll be here in a while.' I said. 'Hush now, sleep.

Brazza and Millis looked at me fearfully. The goddess was back. I didn't know what was worse; having everyone think I was the terrible Queen of the Underworld, or if they knew that I wouldn't be born for another three thousand years.

Usse and Nearchus carried Alexander on board. We settled Alexander as best we could, and then Nearchus pushed the boat out into the current. We were heading south, towards Egypt. We were going to meet Ptolemy Lagos there. I'd had made the decision to trust Alexander's general. Otherwise, we would never make it out of the city alive.

The reason was Roxanne. She'd given orders to her guards to arrest me as soon as Alexander was dead. When that happened, she planned to accuse me of poisoning the king. My children and I would be burned alive. She'd already commanded her priests to ready our funeral pyre. Lysimachus overheard her plot and had the decency to warn me. It hadn't lessened the shock. I hadn't been expecting that.

After the journalist's body was discovered, panic swept through the kingdom. No one knew what to do. For five days the journalist's body would lie alone and forgotten on the deathbed while people milled aimlessly through the city like boats cast adrift, empty-eyed and haggard. Finally, Ptolemy would take the body, have it embalmed, and bring it to Egypt. At least, that's what I had asked him to do, and what I hoped would happen. Alexander's tomb had never been found, so no one would be able to discover that a modern man – complete with an implanted tradiscope and modern fillings – had been substituted for the young king.

The casualties would begin piling up soon after Alexander's funeral. Roxanne would poison Iollas, Alexander's young cupbearer, and Stateira. Since I had fled, she would accuse Iollas of poisoning Alexander. The unfortunate boy would be burned on the pyre meant for me and my children. And Stateira made the fatal mistake of announcing her pregnancy. Poor doomed Stateira. She had been so happy lately. Of all the women, only she had not taken up mourning, believing until the very last that

Alexander would recover.

Sisygambis would die within a week of a broken heart, shutting herself in her room and refusing food or water.

Olympias would kidnap Roxanne and flee to Macedonia to take refuge with Cassander. She counted on Roxanne's unborn child to claim the crown of Macedonia and Greece. Lysimachus too claimed the crown, and he would fight to get Roxanne back. However, after a decade of civil war, Cassander would assassinate Olympias, Roxanne, and her ten year old son.

Babylon fell. All that remained of Alexander's kingdom were black robes, treachery, ashes, and murder.

# Chapter Fourteen

All night we floated downstream. Nearchus sailed the boat, Usse watched over Alexander, and I tried not to think of the future. I was terrified. What I'd done defied all the rules of the Time Travel Institute. If anyone discovered this, I would be erased along with everyone around me. No one had ever defied the Time Senders and gotten away with it. No one. There had been several attempts, but each time the Institute reacted violently, erasing chunks of time along with the time-traveller. This was one of the first lessons I'd learned. But I'd defied the Institute and saved Alexander. I couldn't stop shaking.

'Ashley?' Plexis spoke from the darkness.

'What is it?'

'Is he better?'

'I don't know.'

We leaned against each other. His shoulder was warm. The only sounds came from the water rushing past the hull and the wind in the sails. I thought I would sleep, but I didn't. Hour after hour I sat in the stillness, my eyes unblinking, not seeing anything. Panic about being found out by the Time Senders was making me ill.

Plexis stirred restlessly. 'I just want to tell you that I'll never regret coming with you,' he whispered.

'I want to say the same thing.' Usse spoke up then. He

reached over and took my cold hand in his warm one.

'I'm glad too,' Axiom said. He was sitting by Brazza. The two men were sharing a fragrant pipe. Brazza leaned towards me and touched me gently on the arm. 'I'm glad,' he mouthed.

'And I am glad as well.' It was Alexander. His eyes were still sunken, his cheeks grey, but his voice was clear and his fever had disappeared.

I looked over his head out the porthole where the dawn was just breaking. A pale rose light drew a shimmering line on the horizon. Waves slapped softly on the hull of the boat. Somewhere, deep inside of me, a tight knot of fear began to relax.

'Thank the gods,' I whispered. 'How are you feeling?'

'Not well. I'm having a hard time adjusting to being alive again. I thought I would die. I never felt so sick in my life, even when the arrow pierced my chest. Every bone in my body burned with fever. My head felt as if it would split asunder. I actually wanted to die so the pain would finally end. I thought it would be more merciful.'

'How do you feel now?' Usse leaned over him.

'You both saved me,' he said, smiling wanly. 'I remember I tried to talk to you but no words came out. Was it a dream, or did I really turn to ice?'

'It was real,' I said. 'The cold killed the parasite in your blood. You'll still be weak for a few days, maybe longer. It depends on how seriously you were affected.'

'Who is lying on my deathbed?' he asked, utterly lucid now.

'The man from the Time-Travel Institute. He will be

listed as missing in action. His recorder made it back. I don't think it will change anything. Your interview was a failure anyway.'

'Oh.' He pursed his lips. 'Where are we?'

'On a boat. Nearchus is taking us to Egypt.'

'You had everything planned.' Alexander sounded impressed. 'Thank you.' His smile lit up the boat.

I smiled back at him. 'I'm finished planning now. You're taking over from now on. That will keep you busy.'

'And out of trouble.' He looked out the porthole and I thought he smiled again. Then he closed his eyes and fell asleep.

The sun poured through the porthole. It was early morning. Across the silver expanse of water, we could see the tops of the green trees. We were heading towards Africa and the elephants.

That evening we ate dinner up on deck. Alexander lay on a pallet, and Plexis sat next to him holding his hand. I was restless. My waters had broken and I knew I would start labour soon. I kept getting up to walk around the boat. By tomorrow the baby would be born. I was anxious but not worried; I had confidence in Usse.

To take my mind off the pains, Usse started asking everyone what they wanted to do next. Chirpa and Brazza were looking forward to seeing Alexandria. Paul wanted to see the great pyramids. Nearchus had plans to sail to Ethiopia. Usse was interested in discovering new medicines, and Axiom wanted to visit a place called the Holy Mountain. Millis didn't care as long as he was with us. Plexis said he didn't care either, although he'd heard about great herds of black and white striped horses nobody could tame. Alexander was still dreaming about wild elephants.

'And you, what do you want?' he asked me.

I pointed to my huge belly. 'I want to have a healthy baby. I want to live in a tent, swim in a river, and hunt crocodiles with you. As long as you don't sing,' I added.

Late that night our daughter was born, and we named her Cleopatra. Alexander was infatuated. Brazza washed her in warm wine and smoothed sweet almond oil over her before wrapping her in a soft blanket. Then he handed her to me. I lay back in my bed, exhausted. The birth had been long, but relatively easy. Nothing had torn, my bleeding had stopped, and Usse gave me strong potions to ease the hurt. My new baby was a tiny creature with pink skin and hair like silver frost. When she finished nursing, she fell asleep with a minuscule yawn. Afterwards, Brazza combed my hair and helped me sit up in bed. When I was presentable, I motioned to Usse to let my sons in.

Paul and Chiron crept over and sat next to me. I smiled at them and they grinned back. Plexis knocked timidly and came in; then everyone crowded around to see the new baby. Alexander bent over and kissed me. I tasted the salt of my labour and sweet wine on his lips. I felt light, empty as a husk. It was partly because of the birth, and partly because of relief. Alexander was slowly recovering, and I would feel better soon. The pains of birth were already fading and my emotions would quiet down. I'd forgotten how vulnerable having a baby made me feel. I was thankful for the small boat, for the intimacy of it, and for the comfort of those around me. I held my new baby and slept, and my dreams were as gentle as the rocking of the boat.

The sun rose and fell. The river churned as it met the sea. The breeze reached down into the hold and stirred my hair. I smelled the clean, sharp scent of salt water, the tidal flats, the wide open space of the gulf, and the sun burning the wooden hull of the ship. We had a long voyage ahead of us. Through the Persian Gulf, the Gulf of Oman, through the Indian Ocean, and up the Red Sea. It would take many weeks, but we had all the time in the world.

In the cool of the evening we sat on deck while Axiom prepared our meal in the clay oven.

After dinner, Plexis unrolled the parchment and read The Odyssey to us. Alexander lay on a blanket, his head in my lap. I stroked his forehead with a hand that shook sometimes when I thought of how close I had come to losing him. Paul and Chiron dozed in their hammocks. Brazza rocked Cleopatra in his arms.

We watched as the sun dipped below the sea. For a moment, it seemed as though the sky burst into flame and the sea was a burnished bronze shield. Then the lavender twilight cooled the air. As the night deepened, a trillion stars sparkled in the sky. Alexander pointed out the constellations, and I felt as if all the gods and goddesses in the heavens looked down upon us, while Nearchus sailed our boat through the wine-dark sea.

Proudly published by Accent Press

www.accentpress.co.uk

9 781786 154828